SILENCE
OF THE
CHAGOS

SHENAZ PATEL

SILENCE
OF THE
CHAGOS

*Translated from the French
by Jeffrey Zuckerman*

RESTLESS BOOKS
BROOKLYN, NEW YORK

First published as *Le silence des Chagos*
by Éditions de l'Olivier, Paris, 2005

This work received support from the French Ministry of Foreign
Affairs and the Cultural Services of the French Embassy in the
United States through their publishing assistance program.

First Restless Books paperback edition November 2019

Paperback ISBN: 9781632062345
Library of Congress Control Number: 2018956691

Cover design by Richard Ljoenes
Text design and typesetting by Tetragon, London
Printed in Canada

1 3 5 7 9 10 8 6 4 2

Restless Books, Inc.
232 3rd Street, Suite A101
Brooklyn, NY 11215

www.restlessbooks.org
publisher@restlessbooks.org

To Charlesia, Raymonde, and Désiré,
who entrusted me with their stories.

To all the Chagossians, uprooted and displaced
from their island, to keep the "free world" safe . . .

A STRING OF ISLANDS strewn across the sea. Milky droplets traced in white sand, as if fallen from the languid teat of the Indian peninsula, floating beyond the Maldives.

Chagos. Ensconced within the Indian Ocean, an archipelago balanced precariously along the arched curve of the Mid-Indian Ridge. Rising from the Chagos-Laccadive Plateau are some sixty islets across four atolls. Peros Banhos, Salomon, Egmont, Diego. Diego Garcia.

Evidence of old faults, oceanic upheaval, brutal volcanic eruptions, telluric convulsions that wrenched apart Gondwana, the massive, primitive continent that once had sundered the Indian Ocean from the Pacific, bringing forth the mythical land of Lemuria, which in turn was dismembered, shattered, submerged until all that remained were a few sparse traces, a few islands breaching the sea.

Were the Chagos part of this myth? Do they keep, buried in their bedrock, beneath their coral crowns, the old memory of these tectonic convulsions, of this primordial rift?

The Chagos. An archipelago with a name silken as a caress, fervid as regret, brutal as death . . .

Miles away, nearly straight to the north, another land juts upward. Mountainous, crude, its name a hiss. Afghanistan. A child looks up. A gust of hot air singes the skin of his face. There is nothing up above anymore. Nothing but an incandescent vault that spits out sparks and burning wisps. Beside him, his mother is outstretched, her terrified eyes looking at her legs and feet cast far off, two yards from her body. High above, two dark shapes linger in the sky. One last loop above the heap of blazing rubble, then the B-52s set off again, freed of their bombs, toward the Indian Ocean they would see in just a few minutes, toward their base deep therein, their target Diego Garcia in the Chagos Islands.

Further to the southwest, another child clings to his mother's hand against the railing surrounding the port's captive waters. Behind them, tourists in multicolored hibiscus-print Bermuda shorts pause to decipher a signboard declaring in red letters: PORT LOUIS WELCOMES YOU, BIENVENUE À ÎLE MAURICE.

The child smells the warm pizza from a cardboard box one of them is carrying, its lid showing a pirate brandishing a knife and a fork. He's hungry, too. He tugs at his mother's skirt. She doesn't look at him. Her eyes are lost in the distance, toward the barely visible line back there, where the blue sky slips into the blue sea.

He knows that, tonight, when she talks to him, she'll just say the same words: Chagos. Diego. Deported. Forced exile. Military base. Words that whistle as they strike him, words that he hears without understanding, because they drive her away, because they tear her apart and drown her eyes under so many silent tears sliding down her face toward the bitter creases around her mouth.

He's hungry, and he's tired. They've been there for hours, and there's nothing to see, nothing but this flat, thick water, bereft of the boats that harbor development had pushed farther off, too far to see. The child tugs at his mother's skirt more insistently. She finally tilts her head down at him. A strange fog has blurred her gaze. Little by little, he makes out a shape that stumbles forward at first, draws near, a child's shape, more and more defined, wearing the same shorts as him, bearing his own head, it's him, he's there, in his mother's eyes, but not here, not on this gray quay surrounded by buildings thrust toward the sky. He walks straight ahead, and under his feet is sand, white sand scarcely indented by his toes, and behind him, green palms swaying lazily. He walks straight ahead, he holds out his hand, he knows he'll smile. A sheet of rain erases him. His mother shuts her eyes. And he doesn't know the source of this chasm within her body, it runs from his belly to his guts, and it is filled by an echo from far away. From the depths of the Indian Ocean.

Letan mo ti viv dan Diego
Mo ti kouma payanke dan lezer
Depi mo ape viv dan Moris
Mo amenn lavi kotomidor

When I lived in Diego
I was like a tropicbird in the light
Now I am in Mauritius
I am like a restless bird in the night

—EXCERPT FROM "PAYS NATAL"
[HOMELAND], A SONG COMPOSED
AND SUNG BY THE CHAGOSSIANS
IN EXILE ON MAURITIUS

TRANSLATED BY LAURA JEFFERY
& SARADHA SOOBRAYEN

MAURITIUS, 1968

THE SKY SHOOK THAT DAY. A drum skin struck from within by a powerful, invisible hand. The air was clear, though, just a few clouds tattooed on the infinitely blue canvas. But Charlesia was ready to believe in thunder. Nothing made any sense here. Everything was so different from over there. Even the sun seemed out of place. It always appeared late, just above the line of roofs, and disappeared behind the mountain early in the afternoon, drawing a shadow over the land, like a distant rumble that swallowed up the light. It was forgotten long before it had actually set. Ever since her arrival, she'd always had the distinct impression that it was sunset at noon. Only the suffocating heat reminded her that it was day.

"Listen up! Listen! The cannon blasts!"

The slum around her began to buzz far more insistently than usual. Miselaine, with her hair still in blue and pink curlers and her bosom insistently threatening to pop the buttons off her faded dress, appeared on her doorstep.

"Ou tande, ounn tande Charlesia? Kanon lindepandans . . ."

Yes, Charlesia had heard the Independence Day cannon, so what?

In the dry, dusty little courtyard, the other children chanted their shrill tune like boisterous martins:

"L'île Maurice, in-dé-pen-dan-ce! L'île Maurice, in-dépen-dan-ce!"

There was no way to escape this noise. Here, in any case, there was never any hope of quiet. Whose idea had it been to build a neighborhood up against a mountain? The compact mass of basalt amplified and reverberated everything: the raw sun on this torrid midday, the children's nonstop screams, the deafening cannon blasts, threatening in the unmoving air.

Charlesia sat on a flat stone in front of her doorway. Beneath her legs, which she stretched as she gathered her dress around her knees, the earth etched paths in an ever-changing brown. It had rained for a good part of the afternoon yesterday. The unfaltering rhythm of the water dripping through the gaps of the sheet metal roof, into all the dented pots and pans she'd hurriedly set out to keep all their belongings safe and dry, was still stuck in her head. The water had hurtled down from the mountain, slipped under the sheet metal, and infiltrated their shack. Huddled atop the table with her children, she had watched the pots dance. They had been positioned around the bed before coming under the table, ringing the cabinet, and finally bouncing beside the bed again. Their blackened rims clinked against the iron legs. Once the worst had passed, they'd swept most of the water out with the coconut-leaf brush, but it was still damp inside. A wet-dog smell lingered for several days, strong enough to leave the children snuffling as they slept.

She looked around to find them in this swarm of thin-legged grasshoppers jumping in every direction and waving small red-blue-yellow-green flags. Marco and Kolo were there, shrieking like everyone else, maybe a bit louder than everyone else, and throwing pebbles against the rusted metal separating the last small homes from the muddy stream that flowed down from the mountain.

Mimose was sitting a bit farther off, leaning against a wall. The metallic reverberations from the stones' pounding ought to have been hammering her spine. But she didn't move. Her head hung down and her arms propped up her forehead as she looked at them from below, a defiant, angry fire in her dark eyes. She'd been like that ever since they arrived. Nobody was ever able to make her smile.

Maybe she was just wistful for her plane. She always went there right after school. She would shout her rallying cry of "*Catalina! Catalina!*" and they would hurtle toward the beach in a teeming, energetic horde to encircle the stranded plane on the shore. She was the liveliest one, giving the signal to go, telling everyone their roles and leading her friends with peals of laughter. As they said in Creole, she was a hammer leading an army of nails.

But now she was as listless as a gas-lamp flame that had sputtered out with a quick twist of the knob. She stayed in her corner, huddled tight. Charlesia rubbed her back the way they used to with stubborn tortoises, but to no avail, nothing could make her raise the head she kept obstinately buried between her shoulders. She watched them from a distance, not so much with indifference as with an almost unbearable attentiveness that they could actually feel, a tendril that burrowed under their skin, unfurling a shame that made them even angrier at her, a shame that pushed them apart.

Charlesia watched her. She could see, beneath her steely gaze, the memories whirling within her small skull. She needed to convince Mimose to eat something, she had gotten so thin, but what should she give her? Yesterday's fricasseed butter beans in tomato sauce had gone bad in the heat, a yellowish puke stuck to the pan that even the dogs wouldn't eat. She shouldn't have had any herself. She was trying to get rid of the heartburn itching at her throat with loud burps. Back there, they'd had fresh food aplenty, they never ate the same thing two days in a row. They hadn't lacked for options, and they hadn't needed money to eat.

She slipped her hand into her blouse, pulled out a crumpled blue packet, opened it carefully. Just two and a half cigarettes left. She'd have to make them last. The matches disintegrated against the rough strip of paper in the unbearable humidity. The fourth one finally caught. Charlesia brought it up to her half-cigarette. Her hand shook a bit. The first puff was hard to swallow, with that bitter taste of cold tobacco being lit again and resisting. Nothing like the pleasure of a fresh cigarette. She inhaled long and slow, the smoke opening her throat, entering her lungs, she held it there for a minute, not breathing, keeping it deep inside, then she exhaled a brief puff. Two more drags on the cigarette, then she broke off the gray end with a decisive pinch of two fingernails, put the remaining portion in the blue packet, and stashed it in her blouse. That left her a quarter of a cigarette to smoke later. Yet another thing she'd had to learn here, how to smoke a cigarette in four parts, how to give up the pleasure of that flavorful satisfaction that touched her palate as the cigarette burned down, while she contemplated the sea.

The sea. The sea had been everywhere back there. Behind them, beneath their eyes, the inner sea, the outer sea, its muted, soothing rhythms harmonizing to protect and cradle the horseshoe that was their land.

"Ou tande Charlesia? Vinn ekoute! Kanon lindependans!"

Those busybodies just couldn't stop pestering her. Of course Charlesia could hear it! In this space where every sound ricocheted, resounded, and was amplified in an inverted echo, it was impossible not to hear the Independence Day cannon. She felt like her head was in a drum being banged over and over and over, the stretched skin absorbing and intensifying the blows, scattering them in short bursts that pounded on her eardrums and crashed against the walls of her skull.

Charlesia straightened up. There was too much noise here. The air was too heavy in this slum. This whole mass of metal imprisoning and reinforcing the heat in its ribs, shrill music spewing endlessly from sleepless radios, secondhand mopeds backfiring and choking like asthmatic hens as they spat out smoke that stung everybody's lungs, the sauna-like heat that clung to sleep, this overcrowding that made everyone feel like the entire slum was crammed under their own roof.

She walked into her small shack, grabbed the red headscarf on the bed, and knotted it quickly over her frizzy, sweat-soaked hair. She felt with her toes for the sandals under the wardrobe and went back out without shutting the door.

Miselaine saw her walk by, opened her mouth to ask her where she was going, and, upon seeing Charlesia moving like a sleepwalker, changed her mind. As Charlesia made her way down the slope toward the far end of the slum, Miselaine followed the woman with her gaze before turning around and shrugging in frustration.

"Huh. She really is a halfwit."

She took care not to say it loud enough for Charlesia to hear. She knew better than to cross this tongue sharper and more dangerous than her own.

Charlesia walked at a sluggish pace. Black gunk from the overheated asphalt stuck to her soles. She walked straight ahead, her nose thrust forward, waiting for it to orient her, for it to guide her toward the sea she needed to see. But her compass needle was broken here. Too many smells meant too many obstacles, the thick, rancid oil of the fritter stall on the street corner, the strong odors of rubber and gas emanating from a mechanic's shop a bit further off.

Nothing was right here. Streets with tight curves, cul-de-sacs stopping people in their tracks as they headed downhill. Walking here made no sense. Back there, she had glided down the natural slope of the sand with her eyes shut, the sea before her, the sea behind her, calm and beautiful, caressing and stroking their land like a languid body held close by its lover.

Charlesia walked. At last knew which direction to go. She started to smell it, diffuse, subdued. It was still a long way off. But she was prepared to take the whole day if she had to.

It hit her like a shock, as she made her way past a massive gray-brick building. It was there, so close, right there, on the other side of the long road where cars rushed past, leaving traces of metallic color in their wake. She just had to cross it. She looked to her right, her left, her right again, everything was moving too fast, the cannon burst within the walls of her mind. She shut her eyes, stepped forward. A loud screech, a harsh smell of rubber and asphalt hit her nostrils, a honk, a volley of curses. She opened her eyes. Behind her, the cars were speeding past again. There was just a gate to get past, then a huge stretch of concrete.

"E, kot ou pe ale?"

She didn't stop to tell the man who had jumped out of the sentry box where she was headed. She started walking faster. The end of this quay was where she needed to go. The end of this quay. That was where her boat had to be. Where it must have been. That was where it had disappeared, suddenly, a year ago. Without a trace. Breaking the mirror. Destroying hope.

He'd barely had time to react before she'd slipped through to the other side. If he'd just lowered the volume on his transistor radio, he would have heard her coming. But he didn't want to miss a second of what they were broadcasting about the ceremony over at the Champ de Mars. "This moment, March 12, 1968, is a historical one as our island of Mauritius gains independence," the announcer was saying in a voice that shook slightly.

Historical, that word kept coming up again and again during this broadcast, he wasn't going to miss it, for once he was witnessing capital-H History, he wanted to experience every last bit of this so that he could tell his grandchildren about it one day. "Yes, I was there, well, almost, I'll tell you all about it."

The excitement was great, the moment solemn. Historical. They were both there: the last British governor, Sir John Shaw Rennie, and the first Mauritian prime minister, Sir Seewoosagur Ramgoolam, side by side, watching the British

Union Jack come down and the Mauritian Quadricolor go up. A singular moment. And then the cannon thundered, once, twice, ten times, the mountains surrounding Port Louis echoing each salvo back to the harbor, and the welter of sounds swelled within his sentry box, yes, he was there, in History, he's there, right there. He's exactly where he's supposed to be. Who could have thought that someone might show up here today? She'd taken him completely by surprise. With all that excitement, after all, he hadn't been prepared. He'd seen her poking her foot in between two of the barriers and making her way toward the end of the quay. He should have stopped her, of course. Who knows why he didn't. Something held him back.

The headscarf. The red headscarf she'd wrapped around her hair. He knew it. He recognized that figure. Or was his mind playing tricks on him? It was so hot in the sentry box under the March sun, he'd asked for a fan to be put in such a long time ago. He always felt like his body was leaking during the summer months as sweat just oozed out of his skin, flowing in small rivulets around his temples and down the slope of his neck, along his back all the way to his belt, into the hollows of his bent knees where fiery red rashes kept on breaking out and which he tried to soothe by rubbing them worriedly against his chair.

It couldn't be her. That trailing gait, those slumped shoulders. The other one was fast, she had intensity, she planted her feet firmly on the ground. She had made enough of an impression on him that he couldn't help but keep thinking of her. Maybe that's why he thought he was seeing her now, with the excitement of that day and all that.

But it was her. That red scarf knotted tight in the nape of her sinewy neck. Yes, it was her, the one he'd seen there, last year.

He remembered that morning of 1967 especially well. It was his first day working at the harbor. He had barely slept, afraid that the alarm clock might stop working in the middle of the night, or he might sleep too deeply to hear its ringing. If he missed his first day after having looked for work so long, he would never have forgiven himself. His wife had tossed and turned the whole night beside him. The bed was apparently a double, but what the local cabinetmaker had delivered was far too narrow. There was no way to move without bumping the other's belly or butt. And Jeannine's belly was far bigger now. She was on her third pregnancy, and he'd never seen her so heavy. She complained about it a great deal, especially with the unrelenting heat and humidity. It was stifling and, at night, she kept whining that she couldn't find any position to sleep in. He was forced to sleep practically on the edge so he wouldn't jostle her if he shifted his knees. Double bed, ha! This cabinetmaker must have figured they were both just as wiry as he was. Long as a week, that was how they said it in Creole, and just as thin too. He had to grant that the cabinetmaker had let him buy it on credit, but the fact was that he hadn't delivered any sort of extension for the bed upon the final payment.

All that had been racing around his head for most of the night. He hadn't been able to stop watching the clock. The glow-in-the-dark paint on the minute hand had peeled away, forcing him to lean toward the light from the hallway to see if the hour hand was showing one in the morning, or two, or later than that. He had dropped the accursed alarm clock several times already as he'd groped in the darkness, and had to feel around for the battery that had fallen out. When Jeannine shook him awake, he had jolted. Five o'clock. He still had half an hour, why bother him now?

"Tony."

"Hmm . . ."

"Tony, you have to take me to the hospital."

"Hmmmmm . . ."

"Tony, I'm going into labor, get moving!"

She wasn't the least bit happy that he had refused to accompany her. No, he hadn't really refused. Quite simply, he couldn't. Not today. Not this minute. He had to go to his job at the harbor. You don't miss your first day, she should have understood that.

She had cursed him out, calling him an outright mule and a few other animals besides, before getting in a cab with their neighbor who was squinting after having been woken up so early that her pillow's wrinkles were still imprinted on her fat, round face.

He had arrived right on time for his job, a minute later and he would have been late. His first day, really, she should have understood, he had no choice, not with two children to feed and a third one on the way.

The work seemed easy enough. He was assigned to a sentry box, by the pedestrian entrance, set off from the main entrance where the sagging trucks came and went, laden with huge containers and heavy loads. There weren't very many pedestrians, in fact, just a few brokers who hadn't made their fortunes yet and who were racing toward that moment when they could afford one of those cars that their colleagues showed off with a squeal of the tires.

As he only ever saw men here, he could clearly recall the shock he'd felt when he'd seen her approaching at a brisk pace. A red scarf wrapped around her hair, a flower-print dress buttoned over her breasts, she had stopped just before the sentry box, had set down her wicker basket, blown on her fingers where the handle had imprinted itself, then picked up what she had been carrying with her other hand, leaning the other way for balance. He had to get out of the sentry box to stop her.

"E, kot ou pe ale?"

She looked at him with equal parts surprise and annoyance, like someone unused to being asked where she's going.

"To pa kone?" she shot back.

No, he didn't know. Even though clearly he should have. He was new here. He still didn't know everyone yet. He had to write down who came and who went, pure and simple, that was his job.

"Biro Rogers, mo pe al biro Rogers," she finally said, with evident contempt and impatience.

Oh, yes, the Rogers office. He was about to show her where it was, over to the left, but stopped when he saw her exasperation. She was determined, she knew exactly where she was headed: she made a beeline right for the office.

Charlesia was really starting to get tired of all these Mauritians trying to get in her way. Some time ago, at the hospital, the doctor had said that her husband had recovered fully and that they could go back. It was clear that he was cured, and honestly she was sure that they could have treated him back at home in Diego. A few days of a filao-seed infusion to bring down his hypertension and some fresh coconut milk to clean his body out, and he would have been shipshape. But the nurse there, a man, had been rather worried.

"You should go to Mauritius," he had said. "We can't treat him here anymore, you need to go see a doctor in Mauritius."

He had kept on saying that to Charlesia.

The administrator, too, had urged her to go.

"Go, you need to go, he'll get better care in Mauritius, and besides, you should take advantage of the opportunity, you've worked hard, it's a chance for a little vacation, take the kids, do it, don't worry."

They finally wore her down. She'd packed some pickled fruit and vegetables steeped in large jars of spices and oil and some woven straw mats as gifts for the acquaintances who would host them in Mauritius. They set off on the *Mauritius*, a ship that shared its name with where they eventually disembarked, at the end of this quay that bordered the noisy, dusty city of Port Louis.

That had been more than a month ago, her husband was better now, and it was high time to go back. She had nearly overstayed her hosts' welcome with six children, and their friendship would sour any day now, she knew it. And she wanted to be back home, with no constraints on her movements or hours, no obligations to accommodate other people's habits and preferences. People here lived oddly, always in a rush, crowding together in stifling, rowdy slums. The children were getting fussy, they needed space, their own space. The night before, in her fitful sleep, Mimose had talked about the *Catalina* and her schoolteacher, Miss Léonide, at the school, back there.

This time, they had to give her an answer at the Rogers office. She'd already come twice to ask when the next boat for the Chagos would be. She imagined herself on board, turning her back on this gray port ringed by too-high mountains, taking deep breaths of the sea breeze, a week's calm trip northward, then, one morning, dawn's raking light would illuminate their rosary of islands, scattered across the water like so many sweetly whispered prayers answered at last.

Charlesia pulled a flower-print handkerchief from her blouse, wiped her forehead. She stepped into the office where several ceiling fans sluggishly swept the air, their blades speckled with dust and flyspecks squeaking slowly. Several men were sitting behind green Formica desks with their sleeves rolled up as they contemplated their dirty mugs and piles of folders. Charlesia went straight to the one closest to the door. He tilted his head up, glanced at her.

"Well, look who's here!"

A brief burst of laughter ran through the room. Charlesia stayed ramrod straight.

"Mo le kone kan bato pou ale."

She wasn't asking them to pull a rabbit out of a hat. Just to tell her when the next boat for the Chagos, for her home, was scheduled to leave. The fans groaned a bit louder.

"Mo le kone . . ."

"Oh, just tell her."

The voice came from the back of the room, by the glass door through which another office, a bigger one, could be seen, with massive wood furniture, where an air conditioner was humming. Between two piles of folders, another man kept peering at her out the side of his eyes. But his voice was firm.

"You need to tell her."

A heavy silence settled upon Charlesia. It took root, abruptly, in her bosom, which contracted without any conscious thought on her part. Another voice rang out beside her.

"You can go and tell her yourself."

The man wavered. He twirled his pen between his thick fingers.

"I'm going to ask the boss."

His chair scraped the floor. He knocked once on the glass door, listened for a second, turned the copper handle, and slipped into the office before shutting the door behind him.

Charlesia could see him, he'd barely stepped into the room. Sweat had traced brown squiggles on the back of his beige shirt. He talked for a long while, turning to point to where she was standing. Charlesia waited. The others had gone back to work, leafing through huge folders and clacking away at their typewriters. The man raised his hand again, reached under his collar, rubbed his neck mechanically. Then he shook it in front of him, he seemed to be insisting on something, finally he nodded, turned around, bent down toward the handle, opened the door, and carefully shut it again behind him.

He headed toward his desk. Sat down. The colleague closest to him didn't even look up from the column of numbers he was meticulously checking as he asked:

"So?"

"Well, he told me to tell her."

"Hmm. Maybe you should take her outside. That's quite a handful you've got there!" he said with a chuckle.

Charlesia had the feeling she was supposed to be furious. Were they talking about her? What was all this back-and-forth about? She walked over to the man.

"Ou ena kiksoz pou dir moi?"

He barely looked up at her. Yes, he had something to tell her. Might as well get it over with. It would be noon soon and he needed to hurry up if he wanted to avoid the crowds at the sandwich shop. Yesterday he had to get a cold, rubbery omelet sandwich because the fried chicken liver with onions, his favorite, had been sold out. And in the end, this whole mess had nothing to do with him.

"There's no boat back for you."

He spat the sentence out as his square-cut fingernails snapped shut the metal rings of the folder on his desk. Charlesia didn't move. For a second she was worried that he might catch his fingers between the serrated points of the rings, she could already see the bleeding flesh of his fingers twisting frenetically in the steely clasp that the trembling left hand couldn't quite pull back open. The binder's noise reverberated in her mind. The rings' click, the drawer's slam. He'd told her something but she hadn't heard it properly. She looked at him so he would repeat himself, but he kept on cleaning up his papers. The others got up around him.

Charlesia didn't move. She kept on staring at the man, waiting for him to say his line again.

"There are no more boats back. You'll have to stay here. Zil inn ferme."

He was talking tersely, he'd lowered his head and put his last things in a drawer that he'd then taken care to lock with a key. Charlesia heard the fan's blades shifting the air, slicing it and sending back his last words. Zil inn fer-me, zil inn fer-me.

She blinked. The man walked up to her. Aside from them, the office was deserted. He set his hand firmly on her shoulder, turned her to face the exit. She was outside. He disappeared.

Beyond the quay, the sea called to her. She pushed against the crowd of people headed toward the exit and made her way, step by step, toward the far end of the quay, where she came to a stop. From his sentry box, the attendant watched her, mesmerized by this woman whose red headscarf stood out sharply against the aquamarine background of a glittering sea. He watched her and, he had no idea why, he was reminded of his wife, at the hospital, perhaps in the middle of childbirth, seized by spasms and pain, while he was stuck in a cubbyhole, watching a woman facing the sea who seemed to be waiting. Waiting for what?

A boat. Or rather, the absence of a boat, imprinted on the unmoving retina of a watchwoman. Charlesia stayed there, standing, unwavering. Without even that light tremor that would have betrayed her breathing. A flawed statue, her shoulders slumped, one of them tilted toward a shapeless basket at her feet.

She probed the blue, infinitely blue expanse with all the intensity she could summon forth and marshal from the smallest fibers of her body. Two piercing, fiery pupils that did not blink, that proved equal to the incandescent heat of the Port Louis noon, that started to gleam, that clouded over in a blinding, hot haze. No matter how hard she tried, she couldn't break through the veil, no crack would let through what she desired with all her being. The sea remained obstinately empty. There was no boat, there were no more boats for her.

That's what they had been saying. Just another one of their stupid jokes to while away the time.

No more boats. That didn't mean anything. This sentence didn't make any sense. They'd be better off shutting up than spouting such nonsense.

"Zil inn ferme." That's it, okay, zil inn firme. Her island is closed. What was that supposed to mean? What did that bunch of morons think? That it was a restaurant? Or their office of good-for-nothings? Something with its hours written on the door that opens at nine in the morning and closes at four in the afternoon? They must have been out in the sun too long.

This had dragged on long enough. Her children and husband back in the slum were waiting for her to tell them when they'd be able to get on another boat to go home. The next boat. They wanted to return. She had so much that had been put on hold back there while they were off in Mauritius. They needed to go back. To see their parents and their friends again, pick up where they had left things off, relish the sweetness of evenings again.

The night before, she had woken with a start: she had thought she could hear the resonance of the *makalapo*. It had bewildered her. Nobody here played it. Only the Chagossians knew that instrument. She herself had always been careful around it. When she was a child, she had watched reverently as the *gran dimounn* had made them: getting the tinplate barrels from the stores; burying them in the ground along with a flexible stick that they bent; connecting the two with a string that released a deep reverberation when plucked.

She'd never really liked this instrument. Nobody ever quite trusted it, they had to unhook the wire at dusk. Otherwise, at night, in the garden, spirits would come and play it. She had heard it, one evening when her brother had forgotten to take it apart. She had been perched on the end of her bed, sewing, when her ear had picked up a noise through the open window, light at first, then more distinct, notes that resounded in the calm, fresh air, leaving behind an otherworldly, threatening echo. She'd berated her brother, shouting: "Have you gone mad?" Didn't he know he had to release the makalapo after playing it? Did he want to attract ghosts to their house?

She'd felt the same odd fear last night, when she'd been woken up by that metallic sound she could have recognized anywhere. A makalapo, here, in the middle of the night? She listened for a long while. Nothing followed. Until this morning.

Standing on the quay, Charlesia thought back to this bad omen that had revealed itself to her. She looked at the empty sea and told herself that they'd cut the cord, buried it back there, under the earth that had shaped her feet.

She had a tune in her head. A song she'd launched into the last night of *sega* before departing for Mauritius.

> *La Zirodo, kifer ou ena leker bien dir*
> *Mardi sizer la Zirodo*
> *Kriy pasaze anbarke*

A story from the island. A young boy, in love with an under-age girl, saw her parents putting the girl on the boat for Mauritius. He caused a scene, yelling at the captain, a man named La Giraudeau, for failing to warn him of this early-morning departure. And, in his despair, he had tried to throw himself into the water to follow the boat.

> *Zet lékor*
> *Zenn zan zet to lékor dan dilo*
> *Zet lékor*
> *La Zirodo pa pou viré pou amas li*

But the others had warned him that the boat wouldn't turn around to pick him up. He just had to stay and be consoled by the songs of Tino Rossi, his friend.

If she threw herself into the water, would the boat that had left too soon turn around to find her, to save her, to bring her back home, on the other side of the sea? Charlesia took a step closer to the quay's edge. The oil-slick water splashed against the parapet. The song had died down. Back there, the horizon was blazingly clear. The boat had already crossed it. Without her. And she wondered where this wave suddenly careening in her head had come from.

From his sentry box, Tony watched her. She stood in exactly the same spot she had last year, as rigid as a statue, the fraying fabric of her dress fluttering against her calves, the same red headscarf, tightly knotted, unmoving.

Should she waver, he would be ready to leap into action. She had scared him last time, he'd been sure she was about to jump into the water. She had swayed, suddenly, backward then forward, like a pendulum regaining its momentum in the belly of a long-stopped grandfather clock, he'd had the feeling she was about to fall, completely, without even taking a step forward. She'd frozen again. He'd kept on watching her, hardly daring to approach her. Something in her had kept him from doing so. Her back had been bristling, he could sense it, although he couldn't be sure why, it was too nice, too warm outside for her to feel afraid or cold.

Everybody had left. He would need to lock the barriers soon. The horizon had thinned the sun. He had to head back as well, to the hospital, there hadn't been any news, he had to go see his wife, maybe his new child, he couldn't stay there forever.

She finally turned around, forced her way past the metal barriers stiffly, without looking at him. He hadn't seen her again. Until today. But he'd thought about her often, each time the sun struck the water blindingly enough to render him dizzy, each time a boat docked at the end of the quay, where she had left the imprint of her figure.

Everyone is emotional here, a voice said. He heard the cannon still thundering. The radio went quiet for a brief moment before broadcasting the first notes of the national anthem. A set of brass instruments started off, slowly at first, and rose up in a stomach-tensing, heart-pounding swell.

Tony felt it coming, this emotion the broadcaster had mentioned just now. On his table, next to the radio he was angled toward, stood a photo of his son, his boy, his darling, his love, his life, his small mouth smiling at him, his lively mischievous eyes, his lips revealing his first tooth, one year already, he'd have to start making plans for the birthday party they would have for him.

One year already. He looked up. Gazed at the figure at the end of the quay. One year, and she seemed to have shrunk, to have sunken within herself. He would have liked to walk up to her, touch her shoulder, talk to her. But he couldn't leave the sentry box.

That red headscarf against the blue background: it could have been a painting.

He was right behind her. He stretched his hand out, she turned around suddenly. He was stupefied by the force of her two unreflecting eyes, brimming with a blue and green light flowing toward infinity.

The object of the exercise was to get some rocks which will remain ours; there will be no indigenous population except seagulls who have not yet got a Committee (the Status of Women Committee does not *cover the rights of Birds).*

Unfortunately along with the Birds go some few Tarzans or Men Fridays whose origins are obscure, and who are being hopefully wished on to Mauritius etc.

—PORTION OF A DIPLOMATIC CABLE SENT IN AUGUST 1966 BY THE COLONIAL OFFICE IN LONDON TO THE BRITISH DELEGATION AT THE UNITED NATIONS.

DIEGO GARCIA, 1963

THE BRASS BELL'S ECHOES reverberated for a long while, lingering in the early morning heat, before fading away with one final toll. It was five o'clock, Charlesia stepped down from bed, walked somewhat sleepily toward the shack's door, which she opened just enough to slip outside. The darkness hadn't lifted from the damp land yet. But she didn't need light to get to the adjoining kitchen, her bare feet guiding her the right way despite her closed eyes, four steps before her outstretched hand reached and pushed the metal panel ever so slightly open. The box of matches was in its usual spot, on the shelf above her head. She grabbed it, pulled one match out, touching her finger to the sulfurous end. The flame's sudden glow made her blink. She set a pot full of water on the fire. Wait, the box had almost no straw tea left in it, there was just enough for this morning, she knew she'd forgotten something after going to the store yesterday. It wouldn't be open today, but Clémence or Aurélie could give her some to tide her over until Friday.

The infusion was paler than usual, but it was hot and sweetened the way she liked. She drank it in a single gulp, then handed a cup to her husband, who had just come in.

She put on a dress lying on a chair by the bed, took her hat from the table. In the room next to hers she could hear the children's even breathing. Mimose let out a chuckle. Even in her sleep, she kept on laughing! She had been born exactly eight days after her great-grandmother had died. All their relatives kept saying that she'd inherited the old woman's good humor. Charlesia leaned down, took in the smell of the sleepy, warm cheek, ran her hand over the child's hair, then stepped out to find her husband waiting for her with a lantern in his hand. Their neighbor Noëline would come a bit later, around seven thirty, to wake the children and take them to school along with her own.

Charlesia and her husband hurried to catch up with the other lanterns swaying back and forth along the path toward the center of the island. Every so often, as a lamp's light revealed the presence of newcomers, people would say hello and ask how they were doing:

"Alo, Charlesia, Serge, ki manyer?"

"Korek Rita, twa?"

The flames' dance and their chatter slowly died down, replaced by the wan light rising over the horizon and the birds chirruping in the tall coconut palms.

At five thirty, the usual small crowd clustered around the administrator's office. He showed up right on time, in knee-length shorts and thick calf-length socks, and a helmetlike hat under his arm. More pleasantries were exchanged. The two deputies divided everybody up for the thirty-six types of work on the island. Some were sent to the administrator's house, where his wife would decide whether they'd help with cleaning or with cooking; others would do upkeep in particular parts of the island; a few others would go to plant seeds or feed animals. But most of them were assigned to the coconut plantations, to the drying work, or to the convectors.

Along with fifty other women, Charlesia was sent to help with drying. The day before, they had gathered and piled up hundreds of coconuts, which they now had to husk.

"Ale bann madam, travay large."

They began their well-practiced work. Charlesia took a huge green coconut, raised it high above her head, smashed it swiftly against the cement platform to break it, poured out the water which then flowed down the slope to the sea, wedged her fingers into the crack, forced the hull open even as its fibers resisted before giving way, and set it down with its innards facing up to dry out. Movement after movement. Coconut upon coconut.

"E Charlesia, tann dir toi ki pou fer sega sa samdi la?"

Charlesia looked up. The other women around her had stopped, eagerly waiting for her answer. Yes, she'd like to host the Saturday sega at her place this week. But she isn't sure she can. Her belly is starting to get heavier. She has to take care not to wear herself out. And Serge might have to take on a few extra shifts at the harbor if a new supply shipment does arrive.

The women went back to what they had been doing. The air gradually filled with the green, slightly sweet smell of juicy coconuts as the water evaporated under the sun.

Charlesia reached for one last coconut that had rolled off to the side and cracked it with a firm blow. She exhaled, positioned her feet under her thighs, and pushed herself up from the ground with one hand while dusting off her skirt with the other. She had to take care of several things.

First, she had to go see Serge. She headed toward the convector, following the strong smell of burning coconut fibers. Around the huge, narrow kiln, the men were slaving away in skin-melting, eye-watering heat. Some were endlessly stuffing the huge maw with dried straw, feeding the fire that roasted the nuts to extract its essence, the copra that had given the Chagos their nickname of "oil islands."

Charlesia saw Serge on the other side, his shape blurred by the hazy smoke rising from the kiln.

"Serge, ki to panse si nou fer sega lakaz sa samdi la?"

He pondered. He's always happy to host the sega, but she might do well not to wear herself out too much. And they might not have enough baka and *kalou* to drink, the shortened fermentation time meant neither would be very strong. Charlesia decided to wait and talk to him again later. She headed back to her shack to get her fishing rod.

She had promised her children a nice fish *seraz* tonight. As she walked past the school, she heard them reciting the alphabet in unison with Miss Léonide leading them sternly. She stopped at the window, but Mimose wasn't there. She'd fought against going lately, had claimed that she was too old, that she was bored in this class with children of all ages grouped together, she'd rather be roaming the island. But the administrator had been clear: all children needed to be at school during daytime. Mimose must have made up a story in order to leave, claiming she'd forgotten to bring a small chalkboard or something else.

In any case, she wasn't at school or at the shack. Charlesia looked around, pulled her fishing pole off the wall, thought again, and decided to come in and have a glass of water. She put away a few things the children had left out, then got ready to leave.

She checked every spot she could think of but still couldn't find her hat. She was sure she'd set it in its usual spot when she came in, on the back of the chair by the wall closest to the door. There was no question she'd had it on her head when she left work. It ought to be here.

She asked out loud: "Kot mo sapo?"

A chuckle came from behind the door, it had to be Mimose's, there was no mistaking her playful laugh. And sure enough, she'd taken Charlesia's hat to parade around on the beach with her group. Charlesia decided it was time to weave one just for Mimose, with a wide brim and a pretty ribbon to tie around her neck. She peeked out the window. Mimose was already running off, her hand keeping the too-large hat bouncing on her frizzy head. Charlesia smiled, took the red headscarf that was still on the table, and deftly knotted it over her hair before going out.

On the beach, she set her fishing pole down so she could hike her skirt up a bit. White foam lapped at her ankles. She waded into the warm sea up to her thighs, cast her line, and heard it whistle before hitting the water. She didn't move, she was one with the sea, the fine sand beneath her feet, the sun warming the headscarf cloth. Beyond the green and then blue wave, another white strip could be seen with its band of coconut trees, their island, behind her, before her, a calm, reassuring backdrop. She waited.

The fishing hook sank. She reeled in a little shoemaker spinefoot, its scales mottled gray, thrashing in the raw canvas bag slung along her shoulder. It hadn't had time to wear itself out when it was joined by a magnificent blacktip grouper, at least two pounds, perfect for a delicious bouillabaisse with some bilimbi.

But Charlesia wanted something else. She got out of the water, crossed the strip of earth to get to the other side. The outer waters, where the sea was deeper and the blue darker, filled with an energy from far off, from beyond the horizon, from another world.

In just a few minutes, Charlesia caught three banana fish, her favorite owing to their white, firm meat. That ought to be enough for dinner tonight. She went back up the beach and squatted under the shade of a tacamahac tree. She reached deep into her pocket and pulled out a piece of wood studded with two nails, scraping it efficiently along the gray skin and sending the iridescent scales flying. Some of them stuck to her nails.

Then she walked over to the trees, looking for small coconut buds. She pulled apart the fresh bark, reaching for the youngest inflorescences. Once she was back at her shack, sitting in front of her door, she peeled them, grated them carefully, added some water, crushed it all with her fist then with the flat of her hand, again, and again, like some dough that needed to be pummeled into submission.

Her mind turned to the upcoming baptism of her sister's youngest child. She needed to ask the administrator when the priest was supposed to come from Mauritius. It had been almost a year since his last visit. He ought to be back soon.

The milky juice coated her fingers: it was the right consistency now. She stood up again, threw a few twigs and branches into the space between the four flat stones of the hearth, and struck a match. She waited until she had a proper fire going before setting her round-bottomed *karay* on it. Flames licked the black cast-iron pot and heated it slowly. Charlesia waved her hand over it. As soon as she felt its warmth, she poured in the bowl's contents and stirred the spoon twice. Yes, she needed to talk to her sister soon to plan the details. She still had a bit of the white-satin offcut that her cousin had brought from Mauritius. She could make a nice dress out of it for the baby's church ceremony. There ought to be some pink ribbon at the store. Maybe her own baby would be born before the priest came. Then they could have two baptisms at the same time. The administrator would no doubt give them one of the big, tender, juicy pigs they'd been raising on seedlings and coconut fibers.

A sizzling sound called her back to the hearth. The solids had decomposed, the cream was pooling at the bottom, the oil floated on top. She waited a few seconds, gripped the karay by its handles, and took it off the fire to pour its contents slowly through the tinplate sieve. Beneath it she collected the warm, golden, redolent oil, which she poured back into a bottle. She gave the karay three stirs of the spoon and started frying the fillets of fish, which quivered in the oil as hot bubbles burst here and there, splattering droplets over the browning meat. Then she added a bit of tender, finely grated fresh coconut meat and a few spices.

In the distance she could hear some happy shrieks. School was out, the children hadn't wasted any time, and all five of them came in noisily.

"Mimose kote? Tonn trouv Mimose?"

No, she hadn't seen Mimose, or at least she barely had. When they asked where she was, that was sort of a secret code, a well-rehearsed ritual, because they knew the answer quite well. Charlesia tried to hold them back, but the rowdy gang headed off toward the beach. Only the youngest one hung back, walking up to her, wrapping his arms around her neck, and planting a wet kiss on her cheek before scurrying away, yelling at the others to wait for him. Charlesia watched him running off, thinking about how he was the most affectionate one. She was reminded of her other child who had died three years earlier after a horrible fever. She decided to bring a few flowers next Sunday to the church cemetery.

The aroma of the karay brought her back to the hearth. The seraz was nearly done. She put out the fire and tidied up the bags the children had left all over the room.

"E Charlesia, vinn get sa!"

Serge's voice cut through from outside. Charlesia sighed, set down the bags, stepped out the door. He was there, further down, dragging along a huge skate that he'd just caught with Rosemond and Clément. Charlesia checked to make sure the long tail wasn't still twitching in the air, then she picked up the other fin and helped Serge drag it the rest of the way to their shack. The animal's wingspan, once it was laid flat on the grass, was far greater than Charlesia's outstretched arms. Its slate-gray, white-edged skin was delightfully supple. Serge touched it, squeezed it, measured it. There was enough hide for two nice drums that would reverberate under men's hands and give a rhythm to their next sega evening, and the meat could be shared with their neighbors.

Charlesia left Serge to his work and headed down to the beach. The children were aboard the *Catalina*. The stranded twin-engine plane with its pitiful nose pointed skyward. It fell there one day, she couldn't recall when. Some claimed it had arrived during World War Two, when the British had used Diego as a relay station for telecommunications. Others insisted that the *Catalina* was just a personal plane that had crashed after a wrong turn. She herself had no idea, she simply believed that it had always been there, a part of the landscape, like a fallen tree that children would always climb all over, imitating the engines' roar. Soaring high then sliding along the fuselage corroded by salt and rust. .

Charlesia sat in the sand and watched them play. They emerged from the cockpit then disappeared into some other section like a flock of screeching, joyful birds. The sea had receded, the beach unfurled with a sigh in the pinkish hue of sunset. All the children suddenly jumped down and raced off to the left, toward the tortoise cove. Charlesia got up and ran after them, yelling for them to stop. They'd gorge on the eggs and then they wouldn't be hungry for dinner.

Three huge tortoises were lying in the sand, unmoving. The children circled them, picked one, the plumpest one, and three of them worked to turn it over. It struggled a bit, waving its flat legs back and forth, but ended up falling on its side without any further fight. Beneath where she lay was a beautiful brood of eggs that everyone's hands reached for. Charlesia took one, too. She hefted it, broke it, peeled back the shell, then swallowed it, letting the warm, flavorful liquid glide along the inside of her cheeks. Beside her, Mimose had already swallowed four, the shells forming a small pile beside her. Charlesia stood up, telling them it was time to go back. Serge was waiting for them.

To the left of their shack was a long coconut-fiber twine strung between two poles. Serge had pushed together all the clothes hanging there to dry in order to make space for the skate's hide, which now drooped like a huge gray cape. As he washed his hands at the tap, he said to Charlesia that he was hungry.

She rekindled the fire. The aroma of fish curry mingled with the other smells of the falling night. In front of the door, Serge turned his ear toward some approaching footsteps, preceded by the swaying gleam of a lantern.

"Alo Serge, korek?"

The voice sounded like the deputy from that morning, and the sight of his face confirmed this. His wrinkles, lit from below by the lantern, seemed cavernous. The administrator had told him to let several men know they'd be needed early the next morning to clear the leaves from the coconut groves on the other end of the island. Serge nodded. Charlesia invited the deputy to join them for dinner. She could tell he wanted to. The smell was tempting, an invitation to partake in the karay-fried meal. But he would have to wait to eat with them another night. He needed to go tell the other men.

Charlesia's spoon rang out against the tin plates as she ladled the rich seraz sauce over the heaps of rice. They ate in a semicircle in front of the door, silent as they dreamed of sleep coming, slowing their movements.

DIEGO GARCIA, 1967

THE HUE AND CRY went out very early, not long after the bell that summoned them every morning to the administrator's office, where they would be divided up for the day's work. The air was mild. Charlesia had barely settled in to her place in the drying room and begun to husk her portion of the coconuts when she heard the news that everyone was welcoming with shouts of happiness.

It had been three months since the *Nordvaer*'s last visit, and it had just shown up, just as planned. The men stationed as lookouts in the tallest filao trees along the shore relayed the news of the boat, a minuscule blip on the straight line of the horizon.

"Ship ahoy! Ship ahoy!"

Their yells resounded the whole morning, punctuating the *Nordvaer*'s progress around the curved island to the jetty where it would drop anchor. Over the last few years the captain had come to learn the particular way of approaching the island that the Chagossians called *manœuvrage*. The slowness of this arrival seemed to be an acknowledgment of how long the boat had taken to come back. In this moment, everyone knew that three months had now passed, more or less, and this only mattered in terms of what was coming: a new shipment.

The captain had been especially looking forward to reaching Diego before pushing on to Peros Banhos and Salomon, the two other main atolls of the Chagos Islands. Even his ship had seemed eager, determined to race through these seven or eight days of navigating northward, to the center of the Indian Ocean, halfway to the Mozambique Channel, and now, finally, they were in sight of the Chagos Archipelago, which rose up like a dream come true. With each trip he felt as if he were moving from one world to another, as if he were breathing differently, more easily with each nautical mile toward these islands where, if only he could, he would have loved to stay for far longer than these brief stopovers.

He'd considered trying to find a job ashore, so he could stay there, share in the simple lifestyles of the people he'd come to befriend and admire. But he knew there was a real risk of feeling cooped up. His true home was the sea and the constant promise of land. An intense feeling overwhelmed him every time he smelled the island's scents, a perfume of soil and salt borne by the breeze, so different from the acrid, heavy stench wafting from the continents, too unwieldy for the winds to sweep away.

Even if someone had blindfolded him and put him on the boat without telling him where it was headed, he would have recognized the fragrance of the Chagos. Mauritius, in turn, had a particular smell: sweet like its sugarcane fields stretching, almost monotonously, to the water's edge. And Diego had its own aroma: toasted bark and fresh water, sand and sweat.

From the farthest point he could see that small black dot caught within his telescope's gaze, he had the ineffable feeling of reaching a port he couldn't possibly love more for how provisional it was. A temporariness that could only arise from a belief in its unshakable permanence. A certainty that wasn't quite so resolute today. As he watched the archipelago come into view, he felt a strange twinge in his stomach.

All the same, the ship's arrival always aroused excitement: it foretold celebrations. This morning, the administrator's deputy had chosen the men who would handle the unloading, and they milled around in smaller groups, ready to shoulder the crates and bundles that would comprise the bulk of their provisions for the next three months. The sun pounded down, oiling their bare torsos with gleaming sweat that outlined the firm muscles beneath their dark skin. For two hours they moved like ants in a three-hundred-yard file between the boat's hold and the warehouse, all while joking around and bursting out in laughter.

After he and the administrator had overseen the unloading, the captain waved to a few familiar faces, and climbed back aboard to take care of the usual formalities. The sun was close to the horizon when he came ashore again and headed to the administrator's house. It was custom for him to stay there until the next morning, when he'd make his way onward to Peros Banhos, then Salomon several cable lengths off. With its sloping roof, which covered the attic that boasted two windows with green shutters, the administrator's house stood out among the tiny scrap-metal huts scattered throughout the flat, palm-shaded land. The administrator's wife stood at the front door ready to welcome the captain warmly.

In the year since she had arrived, the blonde woman's skin had tanned from the paleness of a candle. Each time he came, the captain took great joy in talking to this woman who had been aloof and haughty at first before growing friendlier. It was a world of difference from the previous administrator's wife, who he'd considered hopelessly stupid.

The administrator welcomed him with his deep, merry voice, urging him to try his fermented kalou. The first time his men had made him drink that coconut-palm wine, he'd been convinced his tongue and palate were ruined forever. Suspecting it was some sort of test, he'd ignored the aversion he had felt toward the metal cup's overpowering smell of fermented sap in order to drink the whole thing straight up, in one go, as the men laughed and clapped his shoulders. As he tilted his head back, he felt the fire setting his throat ablaze, wondering for half a second if he shouldn't at least try to spit it out straightaway, before the flames reached into his stomach and destroyed his guts. God only knows what could happen. As he gasped, unable to breathe, the others had guffawed as they came to his rescue with some strong slaps on his back. He had been sure he wouldn't survive. As a sign of their respect, so they said, they'd poured him one of their oldest kalous, one that had steeped for more than three months. When he finally caught his breath again, he immediately noticed how his taste buds had awakened, as if they were blossoming within his mouth to better convey the powerful sensations of this unrefined yet ferocious brew. And the heat that lulled his limbs wasn't unpleasant.

Ever since, anytime he searched through the green coconut palms and happened upon an inflorescence of promising proportions, he would order some kalou to be brewed and thereafter his men would make a habit of bringing him a healthy dose. Before it was mature enough to bud and release some smaller coconuts, the men would cut through the lower end of the inflorescence with a special knife, tie a rope to its top, and pull it down to trim it a bit each day, until it began to drip some of the expected sap. They hung tinplate cups to collect the juice and swapped them out three times a day. The women liked to drink it when it had just been harvested, praising its sweetish flavor. The men preferred to wait three or four days for it to ferment into a bitterer, far stronger drink that they enjoyed on Saturday nights.

For the captain, the administrator pulled out a bottle that he'd kept for two months. The two men sat on the porch and sipped a glass of this drink they had to enjoy in moderation. They talked about all manner of things, what had happened on the island, the cyclone that was gathering steam further south in the Indian Ocean and making navigation harder, the price of copra, the latest news from Mauritius.

The captain ran the tip of his finger around the rim of his glass, which emitted an insistent whistle. The news he had brought wasn't good. The conversations around independence had split the population. There had been several reports of violence in the days before he'd left. He'd heard that a rioting crowd had chased a man into a churchyard and killed him. The Muslims and the Creoles were at loggerheads. This time, all signs pointed to an unavoidable clash.

They could hear the administrator's three children giggling; they had come back from the beach a bit earlier, and their freckled faces were thoroughly tanned. They, too, were enjoying their stint here. The outdoors suited them, they were filling up and filling out. Their father listened to them distractedly. He hadn't realized that matters had deteriorated so badly already. He himself was torn. He wondered whether Mauritius wouldn't have done better to remain a British colony rather than hurtling haphazardly toward independence. He contemplated how much credence to grant those naysayers insisting that Mauritius would just end up a part of India.

The captain was still twirling his glass. He was skeptical, but he had to concede that the argument was convincing. A handful of his acquaintances were readying themselves to leave Mauritius and put down roots in Australia. One of his cousins had asked him, almost laughingly, if he would agree to take them on his boat, just in case. He suspected they were overstating the risks. He would rather believe that all would end well. That it was high time to decolonize. That Mauritius was well-established enough to be able to take charge, to be the master of its own destiny. But of course it would be wise for them to have some sort of fallback should matters worsen. A way out. The administrator kept thinking about it. He and his wife had family in France and South Africa. That shouldn't be a problem. But he'd rather not raise any alarms, he'd prefer not to discuss that prospect just now.

On the horizon, the sun was slowly melting into the ocean, momentarily rekindling the light clouds suspended above. One early star had already appeared to the west. Several men went by in silence, their heads beneath an overturned boat they were portaging. The floorboards creaked. A woman brought out a plate of fried fish and set it on the low table between the two men. The administrator held his hand over the crispy skin that was still too hot to be touched.

"Have you told them yet?" the captain asked.

A lizard's squeak filtered through the corner of the roof releasing the day's heat. The administrator brought his glass to his lips, emptied it briskly as he tilted his neck back.

Tell them? What could he tell them? He didn't have any clear information. He was under the impression that the company would cease its operations, and as a result he'd need to plan for this closure by sending them to Mauritius surreptitiously. Explain to them? He'd still need to understand first. In any case, his contract was set to end in a few months. He'd really rather not be the one who had to deliver the bad news.

The captain nodded. In the distance, the sky had clouded over and was mottled like tissue paper. The air was as light as a daydream. The shape of a woman holding a child on her hip moved across his field of vision. She was walking unhurriedly to the back of the administrator's house.

"Rita! Ritaaa? To la?"

The two men heard her voice rising as she neared the house. The child on her hip let out a high-pitched babble. From inside the house came a reply from another woman, who rushed out of the kitchen where she was cooking.

"Wi, Charlesia, mo la mem. Ki to le?"

The captain and the administrator could hear every word of the conversation in the still air. Charlesia had come to see if Rita could watch little Rico tomorrow morning while she went to stock up at the store. Rita replied that normally she would be happy to, but her husband, Selmour, had already planned on going fishing, and since she had to host the sega that evening, she'd have too much on her plate. But she ought to ask Léonce, since she loved Rico and could go pick up her own weekly rations after Charlesia had come back from the store.

The two women kissed each other's cheeks quickly and said goodbye.

Silence had settled in the veranda. The administrator leaned over the small table and poured himself another generous glass of kalou.

"They're having their big sega tomorrow night," he said to the captain. "You should go. It might be your last chance to see it."

In the dusk, a gecko chattered, its chirp like a skeptical click of the tongue.

Seven thirty. Little Rico was lying in his mattress, intently watching a bird bustling in the roof's straw, which was getting hot under the already-risen sun. Charlesia was saved the trouble of looking for Léonce: she was standing at the door. The day before, Rita had passed the message along to Léonce, who didn't need to be asked twice. She never missed a chance to play with Rico, tickling him so she could hear him laugh and kissing his round cheeks with loud smacks.

"Monn fini donn li bwar. Li pa pou soif aster la," Charlesia told Léonce.

Yes, the baby had just finished suckling at her breast, and he probably wouldn't be hungry again for a while. At eighteen months old, he still drank his fill of his mother's milk, but she knew she needed to wean him off soon; his teeth were starting to hurt her.

Charlesia put on her straw hat, took her big woven coconut-leaf bag, and left for the store. As on every Saturday, there was a crowd at the island's only shop. Today's excitement was increased by the prospect of freshly delivered foodstuffs. The shopkeeper was helping Daisy and Éliane up front. Charlesia waited and made small talk with Laurencine, who told her that she was getting ready to move. She and her husband had decided to settle on the end of the eastern arm, where Méa and Augustin used to live. She didn't know where the couple had moved to. Maybe Salomon. Or even Mauritius, apparently they had some family down there. In any case the administrator had said that their shack was available.

The shopkeeper called Charlesia's name and she came to the counter. She held out her bag, which he filled with her rations for the week: ten pounds of rice, five and a half pounds of flour, one pound of lentils, one pound of dal, one pound of salt, two bottles of oil.

"Ou bizin lezot zafer, madam Charlesia?"

She thought for a second. She needed a bar of soap as well. They still had some milk. Definitely tea. And a bit of coffee, she had used up last month's ration for old Wiyem's wake. Cigarettes and matches. The shopkeeper served her, tallied up these last things and recorded it in his ledger. Then he moved to the next in line.

"E missie, ou pa finn blie narien?" Charlesia cut in.

The shopkeeper always teased her, pretending to forget until she reminded him about what she had asked for. She held the bag open again and this time he put in, between the rice and flour, the two liters of wine allotted for her and her husband on Saturdays. It cost one and a half rupees per liter and she knew Serge considered it an extravagance when he only made thirty-five cents for each full day of work. But she'd rather drink it than the baka or kalou, which burned her throat too much. Tonight, she would savor her Mompo wine, so sweet and invigorating on her tongue.

Some men were helping the women carry their bags of provisions. Serge wasn't with them. Charlesia talked to Rosemond.

"Serge kot ete?"

"Li paret inpe fatige. Linn res laba mem."

She hadn't noticed just how exhausted he had looked lately. She had told him not to have too much baka last weekend, but she really should have kept an eye on him. Charlesia hoisted her bag up on her shoulder and made her way back to the shack. Léonce and Rico weren't there anymore; they were on the beach with the children. Serge, however, was lying in bed, curled up on the left side. His loud snoring left no room for doubt. He was deep asleep. Charlesia cursed. The administrator had killed and portioned out a pig this morning, and Serge had left the quarter he was given outside. Now she had to clean it and cut it up herself. He knew she didn't like that. Although he didn't, either. But it had to be done.

She tried to wake him but he groaned that he didn't feel well, and turned over to go back to sleep. Just like that. But of course. She had planned on cooking one of the chickens, along with some leafy *étouffée de brèdes*, but it would be a shame to let the pig go to waste.

Right now, though, she needed to put away the groceries. And darn her underskirt for tonight. Sometime during the last sega at Méa's, it had caught on a nail sticking through a doorframe and torn. She spread the mass of white cotton ticking flat on the children's bed, a good three yards of wispy cloth, found the snag, threaded the needle. She could hear Serge tossing and turning in his bed in the other room. A minute later he got up, walked out to splash his face with water in the yard, and came back. She watched his movements through the window. It was true that he looked somewhat haggard. She needed to make sure he was drinking plenty of fresh coconut water; nothing better for restoring one's innards.

She called out to him: "Ki to gagne?"

"It's nothing, don't worry about it," he mumbled as he made his way toward the kitchen and picked up a big knife. He sat on a flat rock next to the portion of pig and began carving it. But Charlesia saw him rubbing the right side of his stomach with the back of his hand every so often. Well, if it didn't get better she'd take him to have the nurse look at it. He was stubborn enough that she'd have to nag, but in the end he would do as she said.

For now, she took the knife from his hands. "Go on, get some rest," she said, "I'll take care of the pig." No, absolutely not, I'm going to finish what I started. Charlesia stopped and went into the rear courtyard to pluck a few sprigs of thyme and some greens for a nice bouillon to accompany the pork and vegetable fricassee. That should make for a nice dinner before they go to the sega.

The first drumbeats resounded at eight o'clock, as Charlesia and Serge were getting ready to head over to Rita's shack. Swinging lanterns revealed several dozen people all chattering as they made their way to the festivities they would be celebrating until sunrise.

In the yard, several men had lit a straw fire that crackled as it threw off sparks. The whole night, they'd take turns keeping the flames going strong so they could heat their drum skins. In a corner Rita's young son Tonio proudly showed off his instrument. He'd stretched the skin of a beautiful manta ray that he'd caught two weeks earlier. As Oreste had told him to, he'd carefully scrubbed the *raie banda* clean of all salt, let it dry, then he'd moistened it with cold water before wrapping it around the wooden hoop shaped from a thick banyan branch and pulling it taut.

Oreste had learned all the tricks to making the best instruments that resounded and made the air tremble at the lightest touch. Upon coming back from Mauritius, he told them about how, down there, they made something similar called a *ravanne*, but they used goatskin, which vibrated far less when he tapped it. In his eyes, nothing compared to the skate's supple membrane. Tonio had to agree: the last drum he had made, with a donkey hide, was nothing like the one he'd just finished. This one seemed to actually respond to his fingers the minute he'd nailed the skin to the wooden hoop. It reverberated with an odd impatience as he cut the edges at evenly spaced intervals in order to slip the weighty five-cent pieces over the four short iron rods and give the dull sound of every drumbeat a pealing resonance.

"Fer tambour la koze!"

With her strong, carrying voice, Rita declared the night begun. Yes, it was time to make the drums that had been heated over the straw fire speak at last. The drummers gathered in a half circle, the first hand rose up and came down to strike five quick, measured beats on the stretched hide. A brief silence as the vibration rippled outward until it met another invisible membrane under the belly's skin. Then, with a unified and synchronized momentum, the beats surged forth, an outright stampede, the beating took up the whole space, insistently syncopating heartbeats, precipitating a primordial wave within the body's most profound depths. The drums, suddenly, fell silent. Charlesia's voice, ashen and salty, burst from her throat in sharps that soared before dissolving over the listeners' heads.

Bat ou tambour, Nézim bat ou tambour
Ah Nézim bat ou tambour
Nézim dime Wiyem aleéééé . . .

Tann mo la mor pa bizin ki to sagrin
Pa bizin ki to ploré
To a met enn dey pou mo tambour

Tonight they were singing anew this song they had composed weeks ago, for one of their greatest drummers felled by old age. Wiyem didn't want grief or tears. He made them promise to pay the grandest homage they could to his drum, which had been his life. Throughout the wake, between the card games and the rounds of dominoes, they had talked. They had hummed little tunes, a few words. But they had to wait until the period of mourning was done. And so, tonight, at last, they could make good on that promise. They were singing: for Wiyem, for his drum, for their drums seizing their limbs with irrepressible vibrations.

The women stepped forward. Their feet landed flat on the ground, their lower backs curved as their bodies enacted a rhythmic tremor. The onlookers' voices responded. The cadence accelerated. The flared skirts started twirling, sweeping the ground in wide circles as the women's hands lifted them up to reveal the voluminous white underskirts covering their legs down to their ankles.

The tunes followed upon each other in the yard, where the oil lamps' light danced in the night. Everyone took turns going up to the fire to warm the drum skins again as soon as they started to soften. There was no question of breaking the rhythm, or dampening everybody's high spirits. Rita didn't need to be asked twice for more of her famous kalou, which she'd made by mixing lentils and mashed corn kernels, putting it all in a gunnysack, then plucking out the seedlings to let them ferment. Every so often she added some sugar. It was far stronger than baka.

The hours flew by. The sky started to turn pale over the sea. The men let the fire die down in a quiet crackle. One last dance, then it was time for them all to head out together and descend upon the midpoint where they would meet the other group, the one that had gathered at Amelia's the same night on the other arm of the atoll.

"Ale nou ale, nou gete ki sannla inn fer pli zoli fet!"

Amid fits of laughter and joking, the troupe pressed onward to the rhythm of their drums. Yes, every proper Saturday night ended with a friendly spar to decide which side had had the most fun. Soon they would hear the sounds of other drums, accompanied by a burble of voices presuming victory.

The sun weighed down already heavy eyelids. Each group insisted the other wasn't half as good, bragged about their night's exploits, boasted that they'd outdone themselves in ambience.

The only way to decide once and for all was to call the sun to judge one final dance right there and then. The signal to start was accompanied by cheers and shouts of encouragement. The two groups' drums sized each other up, taunted each other, pushed back at each other, and ended up combining in a final conflagration that drew the dancers into a frenzy before casting them out onto the sand, out of breath, practically unable to laugh.

Little by little, they got back up and went their separate ways to their shacks. They had just enough time to change their clothes before they headed to Mass in the little church, where the administrator officiated perfunctorily at the pulpit, in between the priests' occasional visits and more elaborate services.

Charlesia splashed water on her face hurriedly. The children, who had all come home last night once they were starting to feel tired, were now starting to wake up. But what was Serge doing? He knew he needed to get to the tap before the children did, or else they wouldn't be ready in time.

"Serge, kot to ete?" Charlesia called out to him once, then again, but to no avail. He must have been in that deep sleep that comes after a night of sega.

"Serge?" Charlesia stepped inside. Huddled over the edge of the bed, Serge was contorted in pain, his face flushed, his hand gripping his right side.

MAURITIUS, 1973

AT THE PORT'S ENTRANCE, six photos were at eye level on the wall of the sentry box, next to the chair where Tony watched the comings and goings. Six. One for each birthday of his angel. Every so often he imagined that he could have had others. This too-gray wall papered over with their faces. His wife miscarried a year after their little prince was born, and the doctor hadn't minced his words: there would be no more children. But this one he did have made him so happy. "A gift from the heavens": he loved to repeat those words. And his little boy's laughing face did brighten the frame of the sentry box.

The other day, the woman in the red headscarf had told him that the boy was as charming as a Cape canary, but that he must be getting a bit boisterous now. He had to concede that she had practically seen his birth and been there the whole time he'd grown. Seven years had gone by since Tony had first seen her, standing at the far end of the quay, scrutinizing the sea as if she wanted to wrench it open, and she was still there. She always came back, not regularly but constantly. The furrows around her lips had deepened. The threadbare cloth of her red headscarf revealed a few strands of gray, right at the top of her forehead. But her posture hadn't changed. Still the same way of turning her back, like a bristling barbed-wire fence, to the city buzzing behind her. She gave herself over completely to this sea and this sky, as if, at any moment, she could walk right into the water and dissolve into the blue. That was what Tony told himself sometimes, when the heat of the Port Louis summer was so fierce it could have melted his brain.

It was on one such day that he decided at long last to talk to her, to offer her some water. She had stood so long on the quay that it made him sweat just to look at her. She didn't refuse the bottle he held out. A silent agreement of sorts seemed to have been established. He let her enter and leave without any questions. Sometimes he struck up a conversation with her when she was walking out. Nothing serious. Some thoughts about the weather. At first, she had not deigned to respond. Then, she'd allowed a slight nod, a small grunt of agreement, a few words. A yes, a no, a maybe. Until the day he showed her the photos of his little gentleman. It made her smile, or almost did. Her youngest son was a bit like him, just two years older. It became clear that she knew practically everything when it came to children, and he started asking her advice about bronchitis, teething, first nightmares.

And she asked him about the port, its routines, about each boat's arrivals and departures. One day, it must have been in 1969, but he couldn't remember the exact month anymore, she swooped down on him, frenetic.

"Ki ete sa bato la?"

"Ki bato?"

"Sa gro bato dan milie la rad la?"

He sensed that she wanted to know more about this ship that had arrived the day before. The MV *Patris*. It looked like a luxury ship, but he said it was just a vessel for middle-class passengers. An aging liner, with dining rooms, a ballroom, separate swimming pools for adults and children. It had come from Djibouti and was making a stopover in Mauritius on its way east. A gleam shone in her eyes as she asked, "Li pa al Diego sa?"

He had laughed. Diego? No, that boat was certainly not going anywhere near Diego, it wasn't sailing upward, it was going downward, much farther downward, to Australia.

"Lostrali? Ki ete sa?"

She had never heard of it. He explained Australia to her. At least what he understood of it. The place was apparently a new land of plenty where some Mauritians, terrified by independence, had pinned their hopes. For them, staying a resident of a British colony was preferable to a change that, according to some, was just a step along the way to bringing the entire island and its inhabitants under Indian control. The MV *Patris* was carrying a Creole middle class that would rather sell off everything and leave their native land than have to count in rupees. A portion of society that would leave for Australia in order not to risk becoming aborigines in the land of the dodo.

Tony was repeating a line he'd read in a paper, condemning this "ridiculous, unpatriotic" campaign. But Charlesia didn't ask him what "aborigine" meant. In fact, she seemed not to hear him at all, so absorbed was she in the drama unfolding before her eyes.

Because she did not want to miss a second of what was happening, she came back to the quay three days in a row. On the first day, she could see the women with sharp features wearing dark headscarves and the men with overcoats and weary faces walking up and down the lower deck. Those had to be Greeks, Tony told her. The next day was bustling. Small boats full of cases and luggage went back and forth between the quay and the *Patris* all day. Finally came the third day, which was full of farewells. A crowd packed the quay from the earliest hours of the morning. Charlesia was somewhat withdrawn as she took in the hugs, kisses, exhortations, and tears on one side and the excitement on the other, as well as the children chasing each other in every direction. The passengers who had already embarked looked down on the scene from the gangways. Charlesia was struck by the odd combination of sadness and forced optimism in the commotion. She stayed there, a few yards from the waving handkerchiefs and the shouted cries.

Other boats had come and gone. Cargo ships filled with massive containers full of goods. She also saw many Chinese fishing boats riddled with rust lining up along the edge of the harbor. They floated there placidly, hardly in a rush to leave again, just like their straitlaced sailors with brisk gaits and steely gazes as they prowled the red-light district in search of whores. She didn't like those boats. She had the vague feeling that they were filled with too many screams, too many echoes of blows or struggles, which seemed to seep out of the hull, bouncing off the scrap iron of the bridge and landing at last on the jumble of steel masts with no sails hoisted high and no wind driving them onward. They were bits of metal reeking of fish and violence.

But they had not kept her from coming back ever so often, in the belief that maybe, somehow, the *Mauritius* or the *Nordvaer* would surge forth at long last. Today, once again, she was there. She'd heard from a dockworker living in the same slum that a boat from the Chagos had been at the harbor for two days. And that its occupants were unwilling to get off. She rushed to the harbor. The man had been right. It was there. The *Nordvaer*. She would have recognized its white hull and haughty appearance anywhere.

But she couldn't get close; metal barriers stood in her way, and Tony wasn't there. Just men in green battle fatigues refusing to listen.

"Les mo pase. Mo bizin pase!"

Her requests to be allowed past the barriers were in vain; they didn't want to hear any of it. My God, the boat is going to leave again, and she won't be on board, it's going to head off without her, she can't let that happen, she has to find a way to come aboard, she has to, she absolutely has to.

Suddenly, two men showed up to move one of the barriers. They understand, they're going to allow her aboard. But then strong hands pushed her aside as a convoy of trucks entered the quay, headed toward the *Nordvaer*. The barriers were shifted back into place.

Something was about to happen. Charlesia could tell. The men were negotiating. Long minutes went by. Then a woman appeared on the deck. She stepped forward carefully, almost fearfully. She was bent over, holding her chest tight. She seemed to be carrying something in her arms, like a blanket, the way someone might hold . . . My God, a baby! She was clutching a swaddled baby to her breast. Charlesia stared at her. She looked like a woman she once knew. What was her name? Rolande? Rosemonde? No, Raymonde. Yes, that was it. Raymonde. She lived in Salomon, and they had met one day at the Diego infirmary.

Charlesia held fast to the barriers. She wanted to call out to her, talk to her, ask her what was happening, whether she knew anything about her mother and sister-in-law since she'd never gotten to see them again. But the woman hurried into a truck with her baby.

Others followed. Many others. She could hardly believe her eyes, so many men, women and children coming down from the ship. She would never have imagined that so many people could have fit inside. And she noticed that there was barely any baggage. A few bags and hastily tied bundles that failed to hold their contents securely.

The trucks started up, went around through the barriers. Charlesia wanted to block them with her body, but the men rushed forward and held her against the iron bars. The trucks disappeared at the end of the road.

She turned around and saw the *Nordvaer* swaying gently at the end of its mooring rope. The boat seemed so old. The setting sun set the horizon ablaze. This boat would never return to the Chagos again. This Charlesia now knew.

les méduses hantent les chemins
toutes les îles du monde chaussent les cendres de l'illusion
glissent les nuages sur la branche des ténèbres
et voici l'enfant vêtu comme un marin
. . .
l'île se détourne des bateaux qui passent
esquif de pierre sèche sous les sabots de la pluie

jellyfish haunt the paths
all the islands of the world wear the ashes of illusion
and push the clouds onto the branch of darkness
and here is the child dressed as a sailor
. . .
the island turns away from the passing ships
a dry stone skiff under the hooves of the rain

—RIEL DEBARS,
ARCHIPELS DE CARDAMONE,
TRANSLATED BY BELINDA JACK

"NORD, ARE YOU OKAY? Are you seasick?"

Aunt Marlène's question almost immediately set the other women chattering. An explosion of roguish laughter. Pointed sniggers that still carried a trace of tenderness.

Leaning against the mango trees weighed down with too much fruit, Désiré shot them a furious glance. As if to say: not now. As if this heaviness in his stomach wasn't already enough for him to contend with.

They had warned him, after all. Cousin Marjorie might have just had her first communion, but that was no excuse to stuff his face with pastries. Not when they had to share with so many friends and family.

He looked at his cousin in a puffy white dress swinging her basket decorated with gold and white ribbons. It was just too much. She was giving out huge brioches wrapped in beautiful embroidered packets, and she was filling her small purse with envelopes and fluttering red and green bills that the others placed in her hand, looking solemn as they closed her fingers over their gifts. He couldn't count on her sharing. Her habit of taking his things annoyed him, but he wasn't allowed to complain. And he would get in trouble if he did the same in return. One day, when he was big enough, he would show her.

In the meantime, he had grabbed enough brioches already. He could almost taste her absolute unwillingness to share. Usually, he liked the sweet smell of the bergamot they added to the dough. Those were real brioches, he thought, the only ones worthy of the name, a fine crumb with a white cross cut into its top, and none of those grains of sugar that they sprinkled on the imitations they sold in patisseries. Those always made his stomach turn. The mango tree's solidity had no effect on the dizzying sensation, like a merry-go-round, deep within his gut and slowly making its way up to his head.

"Nord! You all right over there, Nordver? Choppy waters ahead?"

Aunt Marlène was unrelenting, everyone's laughter echoing heavily.

He wanted to get up and go, far away from all their jeering, get away from the nauseatingly sweet smell of their glasses full of rum. But he wasn't steady on his legs.

Tania looked at him in bewilderment. She was beautiful in her too-short pink dress, probably a hand-me-down from her big sister. He could see her bony knees covered in scars. She was a total daredevil and as ornery as a mongoose.

"Why do they call you that?"

He could hear her voice as if at a great distance.

"Isn't your name Désiré? Why are they calling you Nord now?"

He met her gaze. She had a brown splotch in the white of her left eye. He'd never seen it this close up. But suddenly it was less distinct, squiggles of light shimmered in front of his eyes. And the merry-go-round seemed to be speeding up. In the whirlwind, her voice still came through:

"Well, are you going to answer me? What's this Nord Vert all about? You always told me it was Désiré. Where did this come from? Talk!"

He had just enough time to get up and run to the end of the yard. He threw up, the spasms painfully long, the smell of bergamot overpowering, on the dry earth.

MAYBE IT HAPPENED LIKE THAT. Or in another way. When people asked, Désiré simply mentioned a hazy past he scarcely remembered. He brought up this recurrent detail of his childhood. His aunts who, every so often, had called him Nordver, or Nord for short.

But not his mother. He didn't have the impression that she'd used this name. He rummaged through his memories. No, he hadn't heard it.

At one point he'd thought it might have been Norbert.

They all had several Christian names to please their parents, step-parents, grandparents, everyone who had had their say when it was time to record the baby's name. Maybe that had been his second name on the certificate. And his family had a tendency to alter pronunciations. But his mother never uttered this name which seemed to upset her whenever others said it. There was nothing definite, just a vague reticence, something that seemed to close her off, distance her a bit.

The first time he'd asked her about this Norbert, the pressure cooker whistling on the fire had called his mother into the kitchen. And his friends had been outside, shouting for him to come fly kites with them. It had been windy that day, and the air currents coming off the mountain promised a beautiful scene. They'd already made the frame with bendy branches and sheets of multicolored tissue paper. He had to get his revenge on the little boy down the street who had cut the string of his Roi des Airs the last time.

He had wavered momentarily. Then he ran out to meet his friends waiting for him, shouting out jeers as they tried to catch the sticks they'd sent flying.

Raymonde had watched them racing off, her eyes somewhat lost. The children's happy chirps. A little girl chasing after them. She yelled for them to wait. She wanted to join them in a game of *gouli*. She'd already found a few thin but sturdy twigs, they'd help her to break them and place them over the hole they'd dug, then she'd take the longest branch, position it at the far end of the hole, *one-two-three*, a quick yank of the wrist would pull up the branches and scatter them all over, and whoever was last to put them back was dead, *ti-rez-vous de-hors*.

A whistle.

Raymonde jolted. The pot let out a long hiss of steam, the smell of dry beans filled the room. The little girl had disappeared and Désiré was nothing more than a small red T-shirt in the corner of the alley. She'll have to teach him this game, the one they'd lost here like so many others.

HE HAD FORGOTTEN. Or pretended to. Only a distant echo. The hazy feeling of closed eyes that couldn't just be opened.

He must have been about twenty when the topic came up again. He thought he could remember a family gathering, most likely a birthday, where all the aunts were gathered together. He'd overheard something that drew him to the lively conversation in the living room, bits and pieces that kept circling around the words "return" and "compensation."

That night, he had been impatient to get back home. Once he was alone with his mother, he had danced around the subject, trying to find the best way to broach it. She hadn't been expecting it. She had gone into the bathroom, had come out ready to go to sleep. She had to work early the next morning, her boss was catering a huge dinner.

"Why do they call me Nordver? Is it Norbert?"

In the sideboard with oversize feet, amid the green teacups and mismatched saucers taken from several tea services, between the cross-country championship trophy and the Coca-Cola glasses she had saved up so many bottle caps to get, an old clock was ticking slowly.

"M'ma, is it Norbert?"

She tried to get around the armchair he was sitting in to get to her room, and bumped into the low table where a plastic conch held aloft by a glassy-eyed cherub was displayed. The silence was palpable in the heavy heat.

"Well? Is it Norbert?"

She turned toward him slowly. In the half darkness, he could barely see her eyes.

"It's Nordvaer."

"Nordvaer?"

"It's a boat."

How absurd of his aunts to call him a boat, another one of their notions. Like the little girl next door who had clipped her eyebrows to look like her mother, they'd decided her nickname was Sosouris because it meant Bat and that was what everyone called her from then on. So Nordvaer was some sort of joke about a boat he didn't remember.

"The *Nordvaer* is a boat," she repeated in a disjointed voice that barely seemed to be speaking to him.

"What about it?"

"The boat where you were born."

It took him a minute to understand what she had just said, in a subdued voice that he didn't recognize at all.

"Born? I was born on a boat? Where was it? Here? On the beach? How? Didn't we have a house?"

He watched his mother's back as she sighed.

"At sea. You were born on a boat at sea. The open sea. And no, we didn't have a house anymore. Or a land. Or anything."

THEY HAD LOST THEIR HOUSE. And their land. That was what she had explained to him. To the degree that she could explain anything when even she herself didn't understand it all. Huge swaths of silence hung over her lips and eyes. The more he asked, the more she withdrew. Her eyes didn't reflect his face anymore. He saw something else there. He wasn't sure what exactly. A slight tremor deep within her pupils, like damp air shimmering above overheated asphalt.

"What's the story about this boat?"

She looked at him. And she wondered. How she should tell him. Where she should start. His birth, the boat, the land, the other land. The real one. The one that spreads outward in her mind and her heart, in her belly and her guts, every night. The land before.

Before fear, incomprehension.

Before loneliness and the sea's wild anguish.

Before the thieving boat that had turned what ought to have been great pleasure into pain.

Before this new land of high, indifferent mountains, of sneering, distant inhabitants.

Before rage.

Before trying to resign herself to keep incomprehension and impotent fury from exploding into madness.

How should she explain to him, her dearest Désiré, about these waters she couldn't hold back?

SHE COULD FEEL IT BREAKING, this portentous water, a damp warmth slipping between her thighs and blooming across the cover beneath her. She knew this signal. But she had hoped. Hoped that this would wait.

The last few weeks, she had walked around with her stomach as big as a globe stretching the shapeless dress she'd made with the last offcut from the island store. A brown cloth that would hide most dirt and marks, brightened up with little beige flowers that spread their petals over her stretched skin.

"Alors, Raymonde, boul pre pou rant dan bit!"

Everybody she saw remarked kindly on her size and shared in her delighted hopes for this moment. She was nearly at term, spending long stretches of time gently stroking her belly, excited and impatient. Amused by the elder women's predictions about whether the baby would be a boy or a girl, which always ended in bursts of laughter. They all knew, deep down, that nature gave as she wished, that all they could do was simply prepare to welcome whatever they were granted.

Raymonde was happy. Her pregnancy had gone by without any problems, like the three before it, and she could feel the baby kicking with an energy that foretold vim and vigor. The nurse and the midwife had assured her that everything was going well, that she had nothing to fear, that they would take care of her. She knew it, all the new mothers got special attention, they were kept at the hospital for eight whole days and fed the best food so they could have plenty of time to rest before going back home with their newborn.

Lately, the administrator had only been assigning her very light work. No longer was she stripping the straw and husk from coconuts in the convector with the other women, just a few small jobs mending clothes or dusting furniture at the administrator's house. Was it because she was moving more slowly? She had the impression that the others were also working at slower rates, that they were being given much less to do.

Maybe this was because the next shipment was delayed. Every so often, the boat came late. The *Zambezia*, the *Mauritius*, and the *Nordvaer* all moved at different speeds, and they weren't safe from the whims of the sea, where they frequently faced cyclones, especially a bit further south.

But this time, the wait was far longer than usual. The store had been empty for months. No more sugar, flour, or rice, the gunny sacks were piled up in a corner like dead skins, the dull smell of dust had taken over from the vibrant smell of foodstuffs. Maybe a boat would come in the next few days, maybe the store would be full soon and they could pick up their weekly rations there.

The administrator didn't say anything. He, too, was seen less and less often. It was fortunate that the island could give them fish and coconuts, that they could draw on their backyard and the chickens they'd raised. But even those resources were being worryingly depleted. Her husband sometimes came back with a freshly caught fish, or some crabs, or a few pounds of a tortoise he was splitting with other families. The last pigs had been eaten. With the vegetables they'd gathered from the garden, she could put together a fricassee with tomato sauce or a seraz with coconut milk. Lately, she'd particularly relished banana fish. The light flesh with a slightly bitter flavor suited spicy bouillabaisse, and the bilimbi and chilies added to it all made it possible to forget, briefly, that they hadn't had rice in a very long time. Dishes that she and her husband shared, sitting in front of their shack, in the sweetness of falling night.

Everything would work out. He kept on saying this in answer to her increasingly insistent questions. She could tell something was happening. Something they didn't want to tell her, because of the state she was in. That was what he was saying to her, that pregnant women tend to exaggerate little things, that everything was fine, that there was no need to worry about anything.

There was change in the air. She saw the crease running across her husband's forehead more and more often, and the muscle that twitched when his jaw clenched. She watched him, sitting on the flat stone that held open the door of their shack, his eyes lost in the distance. He used to be so animated.

Despondency had taken hold of the island over the last months. A muted worry that nobody acknowledged directly, especially not in front of her, even as it seeped through everything, the worried faces of her circle, their actions often withheld as if they didn't realize it, the sky itself which seemed closer than ever. Some of their fellow islanders had left for a few weeks in Mauritius but had not come back, had not sent any news. The boats were increasingly far and few between; they couldn't really measure the time by them anymore. Maybe this was all connected in some way to the presence of these white men wearing uniforms that they were now seeing on the other side of the water at Diego Garcia.

Something was happening. The wind bore vague rumors, which picked at the tall trees and fell to the ground in inchoate particles. But there was no fooling a pregnant woman's instincts, as she kept telling the other women, who invariably told her to stop getting ideas in her head and to pay more attention to the baby soon to be born.

She did think about the baby; she thought about it unceasingly. She imagined it playing in the warm waves that licked the beach at the foot of their shack, clinging to her skirts before going to frolic with the other toddlers. She would give this baby the best of what they had: the best fish its father could bring while it was still wriggling, tortoise oil to make him strong and tough, nights cradled in her gentle arms as they listened to the blurred murmur of the wind and the waves, the stars their eyes could pick out in the velvet-dark sky.

That was what she told herself before the boat came.

The *Nordvaer*. Finally. A neighbor had come to tell her that it was maneuvering so it could dock. She wiped her hands on her dress as she thought to herself how strange this was. Usually the deputy let the men know the boat was coming. They would perch atop the trees, at the island's edge, watching for the moment when a dot would appear on the horizon, off the end of the channel, and they would trumpet it as soon as they could see it coming.

"Ship ahoy! Ship ahoy!"

Their shouts accompanied its slow progress around the strip of land. The bell announced its docking, and the men immediately broke up into groups to streamline its unloading.

That day it had caught them by surprise, surging out of nowhere into the jetty. They almost felt resentful. It had been such a long wait for this furtive arrival that deprived them of their ritual.

All the same, many of them had crowded together. The work of unloading clearly would be far more vital than usual with everything they had run low on in this time. Raymonde wanted to see the big bundles that would signal a return to normalcy.

The minutes felt excruciatingly long. Long. Heavy in the stifling heat of that unyielding morning.

The light movement aboard the boat bore no resemblance to the usual hustle and bustle. She thought she could see the captain standing on the deck, gazing at the island for a long while, looking at them steadily, without making the least gesture, without indicating any recognition of their presence. The *Nordvaer* was unmoving. Silent.

It was on land that the commotion began. A thin noise that grew until it became deafening. A shock wave that brought her to her knees as she looked at the *Nordvaer* and wondered if being so close to term was making her hallucinate.

"Hurry! Hurry! Bizin ale!"

What did they need to hurry for? The laundry could wait a bit, they had been expecting this boat for so long.

"Degaze! Bizin ale!"

They were telling her to go—but where? And where was this voice she'd never heard before coming from?

They had to go. There. Now. Right away. It was an order. No explanation. No discussion. No ifs, ands, or buts. They had to go.

The *Nordvaer* hadn't moved from the dock, its white mass huddled at the end of the jetty like the head of a hammer.

Maybe that was why it had come so quietly, so treacherously. It wouldn't be waiting. They were saying this would be its final trip. And they all had to get on. Every last one of them.

But what about their belongings, their home, where were they going?

One hour. They had one hour. Not a minute more.

A succession of hazy images collapsed in Raymonde's mind. She vaguely remembered everyone racing to their shacks, the frenetic, half-blind rush to try to choose what they would or wouldn't take. Life wasn't as cut-and-dry as a husked coconut. They needed to take everything, but how could they? They didn't even have a suitcase. She had thrown a huge sheet on the ground and filled it with whatever she could lay her hands on. Some clothes, pillows, two pots, the treasures that the children added to the pile, a pearly-white seashell, some filao-seed spinning tops, some kite sticks, the dog . . . The dog?

How could anyone pack up an entire life in one hour?

All they were able to carry, in the end, was a few tied-up baskets, bulging at the seams with the things they'd crammed inside. A whole life in a basket that she used for carrying a week at best, the seven days of rations from the store.

With her husband and her three children, Raymonde had dragged the parcels to the pontoon. All around them were so many lives in bags and poorly tied bundles being dragged through the sand. Muted footfalls, the strange rut they had all carved through the sand, leading them all toward the jetty.

She had let herself be borne by the current. The straw hat in her hand had fallen away. Not a breath of wind. She had turned around to pick it up again. Her husband got there first and leaned down despite the bags tied around his back. As he looked back up, he saw the calm sea offsetting a field of beige flowers that exhaled slowly along the curve of a brown hill.

Raymonde's husband interjected: "You can't do that! Don't you see, she's pregnant?"

Nobody paid him any attention. Nobody even heard him.

"You have no right! Absolutely no right to put her on board!"

His protests bounced off the flat surface of the warm air. The movements around him stopped.

A man in a white uniform rushed toward them and indicated that they were to wait on the beach. Their bags were unwieldy, and they set them down in relief. Sitting on one of the bigger bundles, Raymonde looked at the line of ants headed toward the white boat that reflected the sunlight onto the blue water.

She watched as the flow subsided. Only a few blotches of dark color remained on the jetty: parcels abandoned here and there in wobbly positions. Her eyes showed her strange sights. A *Nordvaer* bristling with outgrowths, a *Nordvaer* pulsating beneath the sun with a muted energy that it could barely contain, like a white tooth weakened by the dulled pain of an abscess deep within its roots. That had to be the sun. The tension. The baby. My God, the baby. They couldn't, they didn't have the right to do this.

It was at that moment that the little man in white came back to her. He gestured for her to follow him. She got up painfully, holding her lower back, sweat had plastered her dress to her legs. She paced behind him. What did they want?

She saw that he was headed toward the hospital. After talking quietly to the nurse, he left Raymonde to be cared for.

The nurse wasn't his usual self as he examined her quickly. His face was withdrawn, his silence heavy. Everything happened very quickly. They were both in a rush to be done. He told her that she could go back out. The little man in white was waiting at the door. He had a brief conversation with the nurse and told Raymonde to follow him.

She walked behind him to the beach, where her husband was waiting with their three children and several bags.

"Go on, take your things and get on the boat! Hurry up! They're waiting for you."

His voice was curt, loud, and sharp. An abrupt order. They hurriedly gathered up their bags on the sand. They climbed aboard, pulling their feet and their possessions from the ground one by one. An officer with a white hat had pulled the man to one side. Raymonde remembers bits of the lines he had said in an urgent voice. International law . . . no right . . . a pregnant woman . . . more than seven months.

Raymonde couldn't understand the little man's response; all she heard was some bluster that betrayed his fury. Then he turned toward her and declared, enunciating each syllable emphatically, "In-a-ny-case-the-nurse-looked-her-o-ver-and-con-firmed-she-can-tra-vel."

The little man went back down. She thought he was going to find the nurse to confirm what he had said. But the minutes went by with nothing happening. The boat was waiting. Maybe the nurse was nowhere to be found. Would the captain decide they couldn't leave without the nurse's confirmation? Maybe he'd tell them that, in the end, no, they couldn't board her and take her like that.

But what would happen if they decided to leave her ashore? Would they bring the others down as well? Would her baby be enough to save them all? A baby, just one, in her belly, her own belly. What if they left her by herself on the island? Her baby, all alone with her, no, they couldn't do that, they didn't have the right.

Raymonde remembers all these burning questions. The boat was waiting. She had been shivering. Her eyes were darkening. She wasn't going to let herself get sick. The children were crying, she needed to take care of them, reassure them, they needed to eat, she hadn't cooked anything.

It was only when she felt a quiver beneath her that she looked up and realized that night had fallen. It was the indication that the *manœuvrage* had begun. The vibration increased quickly, she felt something bracing itself in the depths, the boat jolted, and then it started moving. She had barely had time to stand up before the jetty was already out of sight. Complete darkness. That was all she could see. The filaos and coconut-palm trees were exuding their woody, milky aromas in the twilight.

Later on, she wondered whether that was why the boat had been waiting to start their journey. For night to fall, so they couldn't see what they were leaving behind. So their eyes couldn't etch in their mind one last image of their island, their life.

Half-glimpsed nights and days, murky nausea, bouts of vomiting that turned the confined air of the hold acrid, crying children, and momentary flashes in her mind: images of her shack, my god, she had forgotten to close the door, and the stove, had she made sure it was off, but there was no way it could be on, she had been in the middle of hanging up laundry when the *Nordvaer* had come. They had left the shack in disarray, she hadn't had the time to tidy it up, all their things were scattered everywhere, and she had forgotten, damn it, she had forgotten the doll she had made for her little girl's birthday in a few days, a pretty doll dressed in coconut straw, with a necklace of tiny seashells collected every afternoon on the beach, with its dress sewn from the silk lining of an old skirt that her neighbor had brought back from Mauritius.

Mauritius, she had dreamed of going there one day, she had prepared for that trip so carefully in her mind: what she would bring as gifts for a few acquaintances, pickled limes marinated in oil and saffron, coconut scrubbing brushes to make waxed floors shine, mats woven from dried coconut leaves for picnics beneath the filao trees. It looked like there were also pretty beaches in Mauritius, she would have a chance to see for herself, but the door still seemed to be open, that wasn't possible, she must have shut it, she had to, she's never been in the habit of stopping to close it, the door was never shut at their place, when she went out she just gave the canvas flap a light kick, to keep dogs or overly adventurous red crabs from coming in and making a mess inside, surely she must have done that, but in that case why could she still see the pretty wooden crib that housed a cotton- and coconut-straw mattress that was as soft as could be? She'd taken it out, dusted it, and put it back in a few weeks ago. What if the chickens came through the still-open door to lay their clutch of eggs, and . . .

Eight days. The crossing had taken eight days. They were just about to reach the Seychelles when she felt her water breaking in between her legs.

SHE FOUND HERSELF alone in a narrow cabin, alone with the anguish of knowing her three children were down below, in the hold, without her while she was without anybody as her swollen belly seemed to feel heavier and heavier, pulling her down. Was it an effect of the sea and its dulled motions?

Each wave that hit the *Nordvaer* set off a shock of pain that grew as it moved through her body. Or was it the other way around? Was it the increasingly violent contractions deep within her that moved through her skin, the boat's sides, and spread outward through the water suddenly seized by a spasm?

It was so hot. She was stifling in this cabin. Her dress clung to her skin. She looked at the beige flowers breathing on her belly. They were so pretty. She could almost pluck a bouquet to set on the grave of her ancestors when they were meant to honor the dead. Would she be back in November? In five months, of course. She wouldn't stay in Mauritius for that long. The *Nordvaer* would need to come back, bring them back. But why was she thinking about the dead? My god, did they come here too . . . They couldn't have gotten on the ship with everyone else. It was impossible that they could have dragged all their bones and their souls amid all this hubbub, they couldn't be here. In any case, they held no grudges against her, she visited them each year, she knew just how important it was to put flowers on their grave, she never failed to do so, she would go, of course, the boat absolutely had to bring them back, or were they trying to tell her something, no, no, this couldn't be the moment for her to join them, not already, she was carrying a life within her, it was deep within, she could feel it, wait, feel for yourself, her belly was trembling, this life struggling within her, growing within her, pushing its way out, weight bearing down on her, trying its best to come out.

The flowers trembled. It was suddenly very cold. Had someone opened the porthole? She could see a sun shining through. Beyond that, though, black waters were cast into sharp relief. It had to be like that in the ocean, all who knew it said that it was a strange, mysterious space, as it had to be if the sun could be seen in the night.

Had the sea come in through the porthole? She was soaked.

The waves crashed within the hull, each one coming quicker, faster. The sides of her belly enclosed their assaults, concentrated them, my god, this sea was going to break her back. She no longer had any legs to stand on, her elbows could barely find any purchase on this hard berth, the wave surged forth, receded, bent her over completely as it fought against the boat, against her body, my god, my god, have pity on me.

She couldn't let herself give in to this fury. The sea wants to swallow me up whole, wants to yank my child out of my womb, wants to smash in these walls protecting it, the sea wants to kill us all. Lord, Lord, help us.

Her sister-in-law's face hovered above her. Her worried gaze met hers, as did her shaking hand. Her lower lip trembled as her mouth opened and closed. She said something, but what? The stabbing pain cracked against her ears. She focused on her lips, their distorted movements, nnnnuuuurrrrsssse, that's what she was saying, nurse. He should have already been there, no doctor was on the boat, she had heard the people saying that as they were dragging her out of the hold to carry her into this cabin. He ought to come and look, it was his fault she was here, maybe that was why he didn't dare, but she wouldn't let herself hold that grudge, she couldn't. Someone needed to go find him, he had to be here, he had to come help her. She shouldn't be left there without any help.

A final rip of her flesh, a cry. This was how she finally gave birth.

Borne by this feeling of falling that plunged her into an odd numbness, she looked at the sleeping baby that was breathing so slowly, nestled beside her on the berth nailed to the dark cabin wall, and she thought of the cradle she had prepared for the baby, back there, in their house. The cradle that the chickens might already have taken over.

THE ORDER CAME A LITTLE LATER. Raymonde was dozing as she enveloped her baby in her warmth. The sea had regained its calm, she only felt a vague swaying that rocked them both. She would have liked to stay there for a long time, not moving, not doing anything that might upset this swath of stillness and silence, this respite.

The pause was short-lived. Behind her, she could hear the cabin door opening. She was pulled out of her torpor by some muttering, shaken awake completely when she heard the word "disembark." Who were they talking about?

She wanted to pretend she was still sleeping in order to hear the rest, but someone shook her shoulder. A man's voice whispered that she needed to get up and get ready. Both she and her baby would have to disembark.

Raymonde tried to get up. She thought it was supposed to take far longer to get to Mauritius. She felt like she had just nodded off. The idea of having slipped into unconsciousness unnerved her. But her child was there, curled up by her breast, she could feel him breathing peacefully, his belly rising and falling gently, his heart beating so rhythmically that it slowed her own pounding pulse. All would be okay, the worst had gone past.

They shook her again. They needed to disembark. She felt so weak. Her limbs were shaky, her head heavy. But she thought about how she would get to see her other children and her husband, how she could make sure they were okay, especially the littlest one, who was always getting caught up in her skirts, she must have been so scared, all these sudden changes, this unknown boat, this crossing without her mama. She wanted to see them, touch them, take them into her arms, soothe them by singing their favorite lullaby, she would go down, she would disembark quickly.

The cabin door shut on the man giving them instructions. Her sister-in-law took care of what she could around her.

"Nou'nn fini arive?" Raymonde asked.

"Degaze, bizin desann."

"Nou'nn fini ariv Moris?"

"Moris? Non, nou kot Sesel la."

They were not at Mauritius. They were on the coast of the Seychelles. How was this possible? This wasn't their destination. They had been told that they were going to Mauritius. And why would the men want them to disembark there?

She didn't have time for further questions. The man was back. Two women helped her to get up, a third held her hands out for her baby. No. Nobody would touch her baby.

She leaned down to pick him up. A sudden half-darkness dimmed her gaze, a whirlwind in her mind that sped up, a buzzing that made her ears pulsate. The darkness faded away, she saw the walls of the cabin deforming, distorting, drawing away from her, she was going to fall. Many hands caught her shoulders, she curled up over her baby who she clutched tight to her bosom and her belly.

"We can't move her like this. We need a stretcher."

"You know there isn't one here."

"We can carry her on a bed."

"The door's too narrow, you idiot."

They finally got her out of the cabin, brought her up to the deck, step by step, telling her repeatedly to hurry up. Once she was out, they set her in a lifeboat, her baby huddled tight, and they lowered her.

She had gotten scared because she didn't see her family on the deck, she was terrified of being abandoned on the high seas, with her baby, she hadn't done anything wrong, she hadn't meant to, it just happened, she couldn't have held the baby back, they couldn't hold that against her, they couldn't punish her like that, she wanted to stay on the boat, she hadn't complained, she wouldn't complain, for god's sake, please don't do this.

They hadn't heard her. She had no idea anymore whether she had enough strength to open her mouth and tell them all that. They set her in the tiny boat and lowered it. Inch by inch. Her berth swayed, rocked on its ropes, banged against the hull of the *Nordvaer*, she was going to fall out, she clutched her baby even more tightly and he woke up and cried, they were going to throw her overboard with her baby.

A great shock. Gray all around her and a hard surface behind her back. She's in a boat, a bigger one than the lifeboat. A few minutes later, her husband joined her. He touched her cheek, took the baby in his arms, uncovered the cloth in which she had swaddled her newborn. With a hint of a smile, he reassured her that the children were okay, that he had left them with his sister.

The roar of a motor. Raymonde saw the *Nordvaer*'s flank pulling away. It was leaving them, and their children were aboard. Her husband tried to reassure her. It was anchored. It would wait for them. They had to dock to declare the child's birth.

Raymonde tried to calm herself down. She looked up above. A few clouds lolled in the sky. She wanted to be left alone, not to be touched, not to be moved, so she could sleep and find herself at home, opening the door that she had of course shut in any case, sweeping away the dust that had settled in their absence, tidying the mess they'd left behind in their rush, turning over the mattress in the cradle, patting it several times so it would settle into place, and gently setting her baby within, leaning over him and watching him sleep, dream, and sigh.

"Sex?"

She must have missed something. She was suddenly facing a man talking to her sharply in an office she didn't recognize. He was diligently filling out paperwork in his left hand. An old fan was barely circulating the air. The pen squeaked against the paper. The man raised his head, looked at her momentarily, squinted, or maybe it was just the shadows in this dimly lit room. He asked again:

"Sex?"

Her husband elbowed her. She vaguely realized she was supposed to answer. But what? What did they want?

"Dir li. Garson, tifi?"

"Ki ete?"

"Baba la! Garson, tifi?"

Boy or girl, that was what he wanted to know. Boy or girl? That was what she wanted to know, too. If only to give him an answer so they would leave her alone. She unwrapped the cloth around her sleeping baby, who trembled. A boy. The baby was a boy. The man stared at her. He almost seemed to be hesitating. What did he want? He looked down, went back to writing, asked again:

"Name?"

"Georges Désiré."

That was the name his father had chosen for the baby if it turned out to be a boy. She did not hesitate at all. The man, however, seemed puzzled. Maybe he hadn't heard, she was so weak, she had trouble getting her voice out. He repeated:

"Name?"

She of course repeated what she had said. He went back to writing and didn't look up again. She left the office clutching the sheets of paper he had given her.

They made a detour to the hospital, a doctor examined both the baby and her, he said that the newborn was okay but she had to be careful. She would have liked to rest a bit there, but they didn't give her time to. They took her straight to the harbor. She had to get back aboard, clutching the baby to her chest, and struggling against this feeling of wooziness that overwhelmed her body and her legs.

The small boat glided over the smooth sea. When she opened her eyes again, it was about to pull in at the base of a white cliff imprinted in black letters with the name NORDVAER. They had to endure the grueling ascent in a wobbly lifeboat that sent her heart into her throat with each swing. Finally she was on the deck, then in the cabin. She thought to herself that she might finally get to sleep. But the calm was short-lived. Only a few minutes had gone by when she felt the all-too-familiar tremor beneath her. The boat lifted anchor while revving its motor as if to move away as quickly as possible.

Raymonde reached for the glass of water set beside the berth. Her hand glided across the paper that the man had given her. She unfolded it. Beneath the heading of LA COLONIE DES SEYCHELLES was the declaration of the birth, on June 2, 1973, at 23:30, of Georges Désiré Désir, off the coast of Victoria, on the *Nordvaer*.

She thought she ought to call her husband over, tell him that there was a mistake, that they had to stop the boat, go down again, head back, talk to the man, and ask for another paper. But the noise of the motors overpowered her voice. She tried to get up, but she didn't have the strength to fight the black hole threatening to swallow her up.

She had no idea how many days she had lain in that semi-comatose state, it was the engines stopping that woke her up, she had gotten used to their constant rumbling which had kept her in a soft haze. The silence and the lack of movement had shaken her.

Her sister-in-law came into the cabin, overcome by emotion. They were arriving at Mauritius. Raymonde needed to get ready. She would go take care of the children in the hold, and then would come back to see her.

Raymonde gathered her belongings, swaddled her baby in the cloth. Then she waited. Waited. The boat was quiet for a long while. Nobody came to find her. Had they forgotten her and her child? She was relieved when her husband finally entered the cabin. They weren't going to disembark right away, they were waiting for a guarantee of decent housing before disembarking.

It would be two more days. Interminable hours. On the ship, the children were already getting restless. Why couldn't they get off the boat?

Raymonde and her husband didn't know anyone who

might come find them, to welcome them. Some people had gone down to go see the place where they were supposed to be housed, in Bois Marchand. They had come back furious, declaring the place completely unacceptable. But they wouldn't be able to hold out for long. Raymonde could feel the boat pushing them away with all its force, constricting around them in order to squeeze them out. In the end they were spat out on this quay in Port Louis, on a rainy afternoon. Trucks carried them away, them and their scattered belongings, to set them down a few minutes later in a town of metal shacks: Cité la Cure.

When Raymonde stepped into the one meant for them, she was overwhelmed by a smell of filth and excrement. The terrified children grabbed at her skirt and did not dare to move. In her arms, a smell roused her from her torpor. She had to change the baby's diaper.

She opened the tap. Dry. Next to it, the toilets were blocked. She walked up to the few baskets on the ground, headed to the one where she thought she had packed away the baby's clothes. When she unfolded the diapers, a few grains of sand fell out.

Then Raymonde sat down and sobbed.

RAYMONDE LOOKED AT DÉSIRÉ, standing in front of her, launching his aggressive questions at her. She wondered how she should explain this. How she should make him understand why they didn't rebel, why they didn't fight against this decision to put them on the boat like that, in less than an hour, a handful of minutes that slipped away and that they had no chance of ever getting back. That they could only dream of getting back.

She herself had come to question what they should have done, whether they could have done anything. How should she explain this? Was it a combination of trust, fatalism, obedience? Or was it a latent fear, a feeling of inevitability that had lodged deep within them as they'd come to realize that the island wouldn't be supplied anymore?

She knew that even the strongest winds of fury could not clear away clouds or bring back blue skies. But Désiré wanted the truth. He had insisted on his right to know. So she made an effort. Not to gather her memories. Those would always be there, deep behind her eyelids, within every cell of her skin, they were simply waiting until she stopped moving, until she took a moment in the day's tumult to breathe, and then they would surge forth anew, more vibrant than ever. Not memories, no, beings, places, sensations, feelings far more vivid than her present anesthesia in this valley where her heart beat without any echo.

So Raymonde told. Of the islands where she was born, after her mother, her grandmother, her great-grandmother. Of the Chagos Archipelago, a string of islands scattered across the northern Indian Ocean, in the mildest zone, safe from the cyclones' destructive path. Islands where time flowed unhurriedly, as still and sweet as the milk of a tender coconut.

She only had to think back for her eyes to be lost. Her voice faded. The heavy cotton window curtains dotted with flowers billowed in a breeze that had come down from the mountain. The flowers blossomed, echoing the ones on her dress so many years ago, stretched over her round belly.

LEANING ON THE IRON RAILING that ringed the harbor, Désiré scrutinized the horizon as if it were a blank screen. The images that he wanted to see surging forth blurred together, shimmered, and dissipated in the noon's white glare that erupted light and crushed all color.

Behind him, the city was teeming with hurried people and rumbling cars, with dry dust that stung his nose and eyes.

His chest thrust forward, he stared into the sky, its blue diminishing into yellow far off as it touched the sea. That had to be sand that the wind had sent flying, down there. His sand. His island couldn't be as far as the atlases insisted it was. Surely it had to be there, right there, he saw his mother gazing in that direction every day, from the closed-off end of the deep Vallée des Prêtres. He himself felt trapped beneath this bluish eyelid, one that he wished he could open just a little onto a hereafter refused to him here.

Leaving, straddling the water, crossing the horizon, dismantling this cruelly erected barrier to uncover what it hid, what had been hidden from him, what had been taken away from him, which is to say, what belonged to him, what he had dreamed of while awake and while asleep, ever since his mother had described it to him. He didn't doubt that he would have had work back there, rather than being unemployed and penniless as he was here. Everywhere he went, doors slammed shut the minute they realized who he was. Where he was from.

He was from the Chagos, which meant he was a "Zilwa." Two syllables they spat out, *zil-wa*, with mistrust, contempt, disdain. His mother had warned him. Don't ever say where you're from. We're not welcome here.

But did he actually know where he'd come from? The other Chagossians talked about it as if it were a paradise. A simple, tranquil life that followed the rhythms of the sea, of early wake-ups, of half-days busily working in the coconut groves or in the convectors to make copra, of afternoons spent reeling in fish in abundance, watching the tortoises laying eggs on the beach, sharing everything they made or harvested, dancing to the segas on Saturday nights at one house or another until Sunday morning. All this made him dream. But had life back there really been so simple and agreeable? Or had it merely been an existence that exile and regret had varnished in their memory?

The only way to find out was to go there.

Mauritian men were sometimes hired to carry out construction or maintenance work on Diego, at the military base the Americans had established there. But the Chagossians were blocked outright by the staffing firms. He had trouble understanding why. It was unfair; in fact, they should have been giving Chagossians priority.

Someone explained to him that maybe it was because they were afraid that one of them might run off, take shelter somewhere, anywhere on the island, and refuse to return to Mauritius. They would have much more difficulty expelling someone who was on their own country's soil. But he had trouble believing such an argument. They hadn't hesitated the first time around to deport them en masse, so what could hold them back this time when dealing with just one person? Who could possibly find out what had really happened at this place now shrouded in secrecy?

At the marina by the harbor, British and American navigators, huge tanned men looking laid-back in flip-flops and fringe shorts, their eyes lively beneath their sun-bleached hair, were trading stories about how their paths through the ocean had led them to the Chagos. They rhapsodized about the few weeks they had happily spent as real-life Robinson Crusoes before pushing onward to Mauritius and beyond. Désiré had tried to convince one or two of them to make the trip in the other direction, with him onboard. Their warm camaraderie vanished as soon as they learned that he was Chagossian. They suddenly had a friend or a job or an obligation they needed to take care of somewhere else. Nobody wanted any part of it. If he wanted to see the Chagos, he would have to make it happen himself and get there on his own.

But this sea . . . he needed to understand it. It had seen his birth. It was his cradle. Practically his mother. He needed to feel closer.

But it intimidated him. Was he afraid? He wasn't sure. But he felt an odd unease as he watched it. Maybe he'd grown up too far from it in all this time he'd lived deep within the Vallée des Prêtres.

Perhaps it was angry at him for having lived so long without exploring it, experiencing it. Did he need to tame it? But he didn't know how to begin. Did he need to wait for it to come to him, for it to seek him out? Was that what the tides were meant for? He'd never thought of it that way. He'd never really dreamed about the sea before. He'd never had any reason to think of it. He liked to swim in it every so often with his friends when it was too hot, they took their bikes, one on the seat and the other on the frame, and made their way down to Baie du Tombeau. They were fine with playing around in the shallows, splashing and shouting and trying not to swallow too much water. But he'd never been out on the water, the high seas, borne by the fast-moving currents far beyond the lagoon's basin.

From a distance, Désiré watched the dirty fishing boats heavy with the water they'd taken on along their way here, which the men were bailing over the rust-streaked hulls. He looked more carefully at these vessels that had heretofore gone unnoticed. Started to wonder if maybe he wasn't after all, in a way, part of their family.

Working aboard one of them would make it possible for him to earn some money. Ever since his father's death, four years after they'd come to Mauritius, his mother had been working herself to the bone, taking on two or three domestic jobs each day. She had sacrificed everything to raise her children as a single mother. He barely remembered anything about his father. He had learned that many Chagossians had died shortly after coming here, of what exactly nobody was sure, and people simply said, with evident resignation, that chagrin had carried them away. Yes, that was what the Chagossians insisted, that one acquaintance or another had died of "lasagrin." The same way you could die from too little food or love: one day your heart catches a cold, and you don't have enough strength to bring it back to life. It slowly, steadily dies out.

His father had found work at a construction site where he transported iron to be used for buildings. The work was painful and dangerous, he'd suffered a burn on his shoulder, but the money he'd earned had made it possible to improve their lives somewhat, to buy the materials necessary for building furniture on Sundays. One day he'd had a bout of dizziness on the site. That was all his mother said: dizziness. At that point, he was thirty-five years old.

HIS MOTHER HAD WAVERED when he had told her that he'd gotten work with an offshore fishing company. Something in her gaze had trembled. She herself had never been back at sea, hadn't even gotten close to it.

But she knew he needed to work. It was getting harder and harder to make ends meet, everything kept getting more and more expensive, and the corner store didn't let them pay on credit anymore. Besides, Désiré would hardly be able to plan for the future if he didn't have steady work.

In the days before he left, insomnia gnawed at him. The clock on the living-room wall tolled the hours with a regularity he had never noticed before. He told himself that all would be well, that hundreds of men before him had begun jobs like this one with just as little experience and they had not suffered for it. But it was in vain: he had trouble completely convincing himself. Something deep within kept telling him that, in the end, he wasn't at all like all those other men.

The morning of his first shift, he got up at dawn, stuffed a few things in a bag, gulped down the cup of tea his mother had made him, ignored the warm slice of bread she had slathered with melting butter just the way he liked it. He kissed her, she told him to take good care of himself.

It was too early for the first bus, so he walked to the city center. The garbage truck's revolving light swept an orange gleam across the asphalt of the deserted capital. Before long, Port Louis would be a bustling crossroads, overrun by a welter of cars and trucks racing furiously, recklessly. For now, though, the road belonged to him, and he took the opportunity to linger for a few final moments, taking in the familiar solidity of the ground beneath his soles, rolling around a pebble with the tip of his canvas shoe.

At the harbor, loading had begun. He gave his last name, Désir, waited for the official to find it on the list, took the package of blankets held out to him, and tried to remember the number they'd barked out at him. In the boat, there was a great commotion and nobody paid him any attention.

He tried his best to get his bearings as he was knocked every which way by surly, impatient men. He hadn't imagined the corridors would be so narrow. He had only ever dreamed of the sea in terms of grandeur, space, and light. He found himself boxed into a dimly lit, low-ceilinged space where two men wouldn't be able to get past each other. The cabin was worse, four bunks piled up in an unventilated cubbyhole.

He contemplated disembarking. Then he remembered his mother. His father. He set his bag on the lower bunk. Under his feet, the boat had started moving.

By the time he was back on the deck, Port Louis had been reduced to a few matchsticks in a mountainous bay peering up at the clouds. He didn't have time to linger and contemplate this sight he had never beheld before, because the orders had already come. He followed the boat's movement past the small boats lashed to the deck, fiberglass hulls that hadn't seen a coat of paint in eons. They were tiny, and it was in one of them that he was supposed to confront the wide sea. The mountains had sunk behind the horizon on the other side, the water had swallowed them up. If it could make these massive basalt structures disappear, what could it do to him? He was smaller than an ant on the deck of this tiny boat, where he was being asked to get into one of these skiffs no bigger than a pistachio shell. This was madness.

But he didn't have any choice. He couldn't go back, he had to go all the way, he hadn't been born for nothing, he had been promised a specific, special future, and these were the circumstances that would make it possible.

Désiré was standing on the deck in the heat of a fiery noon where the sea reflected back the sun's sharp glare. He talked to himself endlessly. He was going to set out with other men in one of these skiffs and bring in a miraculous catch. Something spurred him onward, steeled him to leave this skiff and fulfill his dream. He looked at the ocean and its distant limits, with no place for him to dock. What if they got lost? What if a current caught hold of their boat and dragged it out of the ship's sight?

He thought back to the fisher who had drifted for days and nights in his old vessel. He had made the newspaper headlines and the evening news when they found him after weeks on the open sea. He remembered the old man's lived-in look, his sunken face, and, amid the excitement of the crowd that had turned out to welcome him at the harbor, this small figure, which each set of arms passed along to the next with lots of hugs and kisses, laughter and tears. He, too, had seemed to be crying, but not with any tears, his dry eyes gleamed with a strange feverishness. Faraway eyes that reflected an elsewhere tinged with unfathomable anguish.

What had he seen, back there?

And these two other men who had headed out together to fish off the coast of Saint Brandon, a bit further north in the Indian Ocean. It had taken ten long days, and all the national relief operations' resources to find them. Albatros, Frégate, Perle, Sirène: the papers had published maps of the archipelago filled with evocative names. Each successive day meant ever-slimmer chances of finding these men. As they recounted their harrowing journey, they had said that they would eventually go back to fishing. Because they didn't know how to stay ashore. Because, in the slum where they lived, the homes were too small, the noises too overwhelming. Money was too far out of reach. As was the horizon.

A feeling of suffocation tightened his ribcage and his throat as he considered the expanse before him. A vague unease, an indistinct narrowing of his respiratory tracts as he tried to take in gulps of this immense space in front of him. Désiré looked away, went back below deck. He would feel better soon, he shouldn't push himself too far.

The sea, he knew, wasn't some sort of swimming pool where anyone could jump in and splash a bit. Here, the sea was imperious, it held the power, it shaped space and slowed time, amplifying this experience of the infinitesimal, the better to command respect for its sheer size. It lazily numbed the senses in order to overwhelm them with its essence, its mineral components which would eventually explode in an ecstasy that the earth scarcely hinted at.

Désiré told himself all this. He had to resist this insidious fear closing in on his stomach, nothing could ruin his reunion, he just had to be patient and calm, yes, that was what the sea taught, humility and patience, it was worth that, he knew it, he would do what it took. He would wait for night to fall. The hubbub of men around him would subside, would quiet down, he could finally experience this long-awaited communion with the sea.

But the evening came and the sun cast a dark sheen on the sky as it descended into the water, without taming the tempest on board. Where could he find any quiet on this boat that kept on twitching and jolting like a bumblebee in a bowl?

Désiré didn't feel well. An unpleasant smell of thawing fish followed him into every nook. The sea had changed. It set the boat swaying and pounded deep within his body. It loosened the planks beneath his feet.

Four strong hands pulled him back up, dragged him to his cabin, and left him there amid sneering laughter.

Curled up in the narrow berth, he tried to push away the nausea deep within his guts. Maybe he would feel better if he lay on his stomach. No, that was actually worse, the mattress pressing on his belly made him feel even more nauseous. He turned on his side, a heavy stupor slowly came over him. Maybe he would be able to sleep at last. He clung to this thought like a life preserver. This sluggishness inflating and deflating his stomach in rubbery waves would keep him above water. As he kept his cheek pressed against the flat pillow, a stifling feeling rose in his throat. No, he needed to stop this movement. Maybe it'd be better on his back, maybe that might relieve the pressure on his belly. But shifting would take such effort. He had to convince himself first. Yes, he needed to turn over, it was better to try something, anything, to stop this sluggish turbulence in his guts.

He pushed with his lower back, shifted his body slowly, his right leg bent, his foot flat, his hip, a moment to reach for his shoulder, a twist, and all the rest followed. He breathed deeply now that his belly was freed, sighed, tried to slow his breathing. He wanted to believe in this little bit of relief.

But his shut eyes only made it easier for his thoughts to circle around this cyclone gaining steam within his gut. He had to open his eyes, quickly, and fix them on something that could steady him. Above him, the narrow wooden planks of the upper bunk began to sway. It was lowering, it was coming closer, it was going to crush him. His fear gave him enough strength to stumble off the mattress, his body falling with a heavy thud. A bomb was pulverizing the sides of his skull.

The bed was going to fall on him, the bed was going to fall on him, that was all he had the energy to whimper to the sailor who was picking him up. Higher, he wanted to be higher up, on the upper bunk. That way he wouldn't have a bed above him. That would be better. That ought to be better. He just needed to summon his strength one last time. Help me. His two elbows dug into the thin mattress, his leg muscles refused to move, just one push, they were there, they couldn't have given out so quickly, it was just his willpower that had gone, he couldn't be that lazy, he had to pull himself together, get himself up, just one push, yes, there, his thigh was tensing, yes, he needed to hold onto that, make that tension move to his calf, lower down, to his feet, where were they, they ought to have been right there even though he couldn't feel them anymore, he couldn't have lost them, they absolutely had to be there, an extension of this long, inchoate pain that he knew to be his legs.

The sailor was losing patience. Another attempt. Désiré could feel the faint pins and needles that indicated blood was moving through his body. Another grunt and thrust and then he was on the upper bunk. At last. A little distance between him and this sea that felt too close to his body. This sea that thundered through him even as its surface was barely disturbed by a few eddies. The fact that it had brought him into the world must have been why he felt its motion so keenly within himself. Maybe this was its way of welcoming him and telling him that it knew him, its way of taking him into its arms and cradling him.

If only it could have stilled his intestines' slow upheaval, just for a moment, a long moment, until the ship was safely in the harbor and he could climb back onto the deck to see it again, scrutinize it in the gauzy light of sunrise and in the blazing fire of sunset, so he could see how beautiful it was and love it, so he could feel like he was one with the sea, so he could reap its fluidity and its strength, tell it what had become of him since they first met. So that he would have time to tell it about his mother, maybe it remembered her. His mother back there, all alone, her face came to him, imprinted with deep sadness. Would he really see her again?

The whole sea flowed through his veins. It welled up in his eyes and fell in salty droplets. He needed to get a hold on himself, he knew it, his path couldn't end here, that made no sense at all.

With his eyes shut, he tried to regain control of his breathing. To soothe the pounding of his blood in his temples, to slow the thudding of the wild animal in his torso. To stop this interminable swaying in his head.

This boat was going to sink.

Maybe that was his fate. To reach the bottom of the ocean where he was born, to die there. A boat, his cradle, his grave.

But it was land he was looking for. His land. This sea could not be his home, it didn't want him, a motherland never turns its back on its children. They must have been making things up, he wasn't born on the sea, its smell did not awaken any of his senses, he didn't know its rhythms, he feared falling with every step. He could lick his lips and that taste would not remind him of anything. Just a vague memory of his mother's kitchen, when she was breading and frying the salted fish he always thought was so bitter that he pushed it to the edge of his plate or hid it beneath a bit of rice so she wouldn't see.

He didn't know this sea. It didn't acknowledge him. It didn't accept him.

And so it was unleashing its ill will against him today, it wanted his flesh, he had to push back, it couldn't just have whatever it wanted, he had to escape it, he understood now why his mother lived so far away from it, she knew all too well its treachery, its false camaraderie which masked the dark waves relentlessly pummeling him and sometimes dragging him under, rising up in tidal waves and furious tempests.

He saw it, he foresaw its underhandedness, it would dissolve him from the inside out, insidiously, it would leach his ribs and his spine, liquefy his stomach and his viscera, all that would be left was its water, spilling from the wineskin that was his flesh.

He barely had time to heave his torso out of the bunk. He vomited a long while, feverishly, onto the cabin floor, wondering where this smell of bergamot filling his throat and his head had come from.

THE SEA HADN'T WANTED HIM, and so he had ended up back on land. For weeks, he had been scanning the classifieds in the major papers every day. Rows of close-set letters that started moving like lines of black ants beneath his weary eyes. Nothing but jobs as factory engineers or other roles that required experience he didn't have. He was going in circles.

A friend told him about a big construction company that was looking for builders at various construction sites, and he didn't hesitate. Two days later, Désiré was hired.

The work uniform they had given him added a certain look to his frame. But as soon as he stepped onto the construction site, the enthusiasm he had tried to muster deflated like a soufflé.

Grayness swiftly closed in around him. The already tall tower obscured the sky, iron rods were sticking out of all the cold concrete, and the cement dust coated the sparse grasses and the men's hair. A few yellow hemispheres stood out: only the important-looking men who visited the site on occasion to point out things and bark out orders wore safety helmets.

Désiré had jolted when a tremor had begun, not beneath his feet, but up in the air. A metallic rumble, punctuated by occasional sounds of scraping that reminded him of the noise a lawn mower made when hitting a pebble. The cement mixers had started working. Their revolutions would set the whole day's rhythm, with only half an hour's rest during the lunch break.

The cement dust clung to his body, its acidity ate away at his skin. The grayness choked his muscles and his will-power.

Désiré sat at the table for dinner with no appetite at all. A shooting pain ran through his shoulder. He would have to go back tomorrow, and the next day, and beyond. He would have to force his crippled body to get up each morning, to pull on his uniform stiffened by a nearly invisible coating of cement dust to the point of standing upright on its own, piling up bricks, feeling their rough surface beneath his hands, the concrete mixers tirelessly spitting their thick, gray sludge, the men talking loudly when the machines had stopped, yelling at each other from opposite ends of the site, shouting jokes at the top of their voices that he could only hear parts of as they burst into riotous laughter.

He wasn't made for this wordless drudgery of laying concrete. But what else are you going to do? another voice had asked him. Run away? Go to sea? You already tried that and came back, didn't you? The sea didn't want you, it spat you back out like a bit of kelp. Yes, he remembered perfectly. His washing up like a shipwreck. His refusal to go back to sea. Never again. He had barely come out alive. He wasn't going to risk it a second time. There were plenty of men born on land who never felt at home on the high seas, after all. So he would go back to the construction site. The next day, and all the days after that.

On the third day of work, the foreman told him that the company paid their salaries directly into their employees' bank accounts. He needed one. A bank account. The prospect delighted him. He would have money, more than his pockets could hold. The following day, he went to the center of Port Louis.

The revolving doors had given him pause, until he was able to follow right behind a man in a tie walking briskly. The long row of bank counters under fluorescent light wasn't reassuring. He watched account holders moving from one counter to the next, asked a uniformed employee where to go. He was directed toward a young woman who he understood was in charge of opening new accounts.

She barely glanced at him. Her attention was on the form she had taken out of a drawer and was filling out in triplicate, white, blue, and yellow. First name. Last name. Date of birth. ID card.

Désiré fell silent.

"ID card, please." Her voice became more insistent, with a hint of impatience.

He walked out of the bank a few minutes later, distraught. He didn't have an ID card.

The next day, the news landed like a hammer blow from the Social Security office. He couldn't obtain a national ID card. He wasn't Mauritian.

"See, it's written on your birth certificate: born on the *Vordvaer* off the coast of the Seychelles."

"Not *Vordvaer*. *Nordvaer*."

"What?"

"There's a mistake on the paper, they wrote wrong. It should say born on the *Nordvaer*, not the *Vordvaer*."

"All right. Fine. As you wish. In any case we can't give you an ID card."

That was that. The Social Security officer seemed not to be surprised at all.

Désiré, however, hadn't seen the last of his troubles. His birth certificate was riddled with errors. "Georges Désiré Désir" was written on it. Désir being the last name, even though his entire family was called Désiré. What had the registrar in the Seychelles been thinking?

He had to go see lawyers, swear affidavits, and undertake a long succession of complicated, costly procedures. It was only after the Prime Minister's office interceded that he finally received a provisional ID card. But his two days' salary were gone. He hadn't gone back to the construction site.

Désiré didn't know where he belonged anymore. Mauritius? He had always lived here but he had no nationality. The Seychelles? He had never seen that land. Britain? They were even less willing to take him on there. The Chagos? He had never been to those islands where he should have come into the world. His place of birth was a boat that had disappeared.

DÉSIRÉ WAS ALMOST DISAPPOINTED. He had imagined something sizable, a foreboding silhouette, a bit like that of a slave ship, a dark, imposing mass that contained a world of anguish, pain, agony. More than a century after slavery had been officially abolished, the Chagossians had still been treated as such, crammed into holds, unloaded on a quay, cast aside without any further thought in hopes that they might simply disperse into a brownish dust that the lightest sea breeze would carry away.

The *Nordvaer* bore no resemblance to all the hideous or sinister depictions he had envisioned. The photo showed a boat that was completely white, absolutely unremarkable. Down to its size, so modest that he had trouble believing it had indeed transported so many souls. There must have been a mistake.

Then Désiré had the idea to write to the National Library of Norway, an idea that ultimately paid off. After several letters had been exchanged with staff members up to its director, he had a number of consistent pieces of information. And a letter.

The envelope was all crumpled up, somewhat dented with a tear on one side. He ripped the brown paper hastily and pulled out a wad of printed sheets. A copy of an article on the *Nordvaer* written by T. G. Bodegaard, which had been published in a shipping newsletter.

"Dinner is ready."

His mother's voice. She was right behind the curtain separating his bedroom from the living room. Désiré slid the envelope under his pillow and stepped out. In the kitchen, on the plastic tablecloth with geometric patterns, she had set down plates of steaming rice. They ate in silence as they listened to music on the radio. Désiré could tell that his mother was waiting for him to talk. But he was too eager to read the article; he picked at his plate, got up, and went outside to give his leftovers to the dog.

The chain was broken. It was dangling all alone by the low wall bordering the neighbors' yard. The dog had found some way to escape. Désiré spent the whole night roaming the neighborhood in hopes of finding his pet again. Around midnight, he found the dog at last, fidgeting beside a door. It could smell a bitch on the other side. Bringing the animal back was no easy feat.

It was nearly one in the morning when Désiré finally lay down on his bed with the precious envelope in his hand. He was exhausted enough that it took serious effort to focus on the letters blurring in front of his eyes.

. . .

He carried these screams within his frame. They reverberated in his carcass, their dulled waves scaring off the birds that happened to perch on him. He tried in vain to withdraw into the sand he was already sinking into, but these strange vibrations that sundered waters began again. All it took was a bird's shriek for silence to be shattered within his old body.

Reawakened, abruptly. They were there. All of them. Tens and hundreds of them clinging to him, pushing him away, trying to flee him, but forced to lean against his walls in hopes of breathing, of escaping the pressure of other bodies, so many other teetering, colliding bodies.

He never could have believed this. That he could carry so many bodies and not burst. But he had had the time to test his limits over innumerable voyages. Built in Elmshorn, near Hamburg, he had made his first trips for a navigation company on the coast of Bodø. In Norway.

1958. A year of note. Each week he traveled between Trondheim and the Lofoten Islands. An agreeable job: ferrying passengers, usually refined British visitors, no more than a dozen, one way. And carrying a load of freshly caught fish and seafood the other way. He took such pride in connecting these islands with the stark, arrogant mountains. Ah, this haughty nature, this cold yet living sea. It had been nothing like here. Nobody had cared about the shock he had sustained in becoming unmoored from his homeland, about the suffocation he had endured the first time he had entered these warm, salty, heavy waters of the South.

Years went by coming and going without the least hiccup, without a single delay. Then things changed. First was the train: the arrival of trains had made him useless. This heavy, noisy, dirty railroad had replaced him summarily.

Humanity's ingratitude had sold him to the other end of the world. To the Seychellois government. His first voyage had been a nightmare. He had thought he would fall apart in crossing the equator. But he was possessed of a solid constitution. He had become habituated, and even learned to take pleasure in being there. To be sure, this was another existence; he sailed around the Indian Ocean, between Mauritius, the Seychelles, and the Chagos, transporting provisions and coconut-palm derivatives including oil, brooms, and brushes, as well as the occasional passenger. He had become valuable again, keenly anticipated, and he came to appreciate the temperament of these warmer, happier people he cared for.

At the end of the sixties, he had been emblematized on a stamp that was printed in honor of the anniversary of the British Indian Ocean Territories. This famous BIOT that grouped together the British colonies of the Indian Ocean. With the profile of the Queen of England watching over him from above on the right side of the small square of paper. He and the Queen, together in the same frame. This felt worth the pain of having left his Norwegian waters.

He had to undergo some repairs thereafter. No doubt they had grander ambitions for him, because the addition of an upper deck had, in a single move, dramatically increased his capacity. His profile had changed, of course, but he was eager to discover the even more glorious future that had been envisioned for him.

He had begun to pick up odd rumors on board. The details became much clearer one night in the middle of one of his crossings. He had heard them talking. Forcibly removing these people he had grown accustomed to? He refused to help in any way with this expulsion. A cyclone, a storm, a murky groundswell would come and capsize him and free him of these conspirators, eject them, drown them, them and their evil plans too.

But he was powerless.

They had loaded him to the brim with poorly tied bags, men, women, children, piled up every which way. He would have liked to swell up, make himself bigger, give them a little more space, but he had no way to, he had no idea how to.

During the entire crossing he remembered, almost ritualistically, the words of Norway's national anthem. *Ja, vi elsker dette landet. Yes, we love, with fond devotion, this our land.* If there were an image of death, it might have been these distant, flowing memories. It might have been the warnings that he would sink, dragged downward by the weight of all these people, the weight of the despair crushing them in his hold.

He remembered a dog that had chased after him, barking behind him, and a child that he had carried on his deck, the child holding out its hand, both its hands, holding out its cries and its entire body to the dog. The dog had run on three legs, nearly dislocating its ribs, running on three legs with a wild energy, this need that did not relent, did not waver. This dog that pursued him, the ship carrying away this child like a thief.

The dog had run alongside his wake and followed him so long as there was sand beneath its paws. Suddenly the dog had stopped, brought up short by the sea. And had watched him leaving, standing on its three paws, a dramatic, ludicrous silhouette, a final sentry that no longer had anything to guard. Nor anything to hope for.

He did not know how long the dog had stayed there after he had fallen out of sight, a dot that could just as easily have been a bird perched on a fading memory of land. Whether it had gone to sleep there, at that spot, or if it had turned back, its head lowered. If it had survived, for how long. How. With three legs and no eyes. These eyes he had carried, could still feel, embedded in his hull, on his starboard side. Everywhere, he had carried them everywhere, across the seas, as far as he could flee, he had even dreamed of drowning them, of drowning himself, but to no avail. And all this water that washed him every day without protecting him. These eyes burned him, two blowtorches that bore through his sides, that drilled through his shell to reach his core.

He had heard them talking, in the captain's cabin, about how they had killed them all before he had arrived. All the dogs. They had rounded them all up. Some had tried to escape. They hadn't made it far. Beaten into submission with baton blows. Shoved into the convectors. They had shut the door. Filled the oven's maw with dry straw. Started the fire.

He knew he had seen this dog, a survivor no doubt. Those eyes of its remained, howling even more loudly than a dog that could smell death coming, with far more insistence, more despair. And these howls mixed with the screams, silent screams shut away in human throats, screams that never rang out because they couldn't make it past clenched jaws or pressed lips.

But he had heard them. Hoarse, raw, bristling with fear and incomprehension.

He had never stopped hearing them, no storm had ever silenced them.

They resounded within him, the silent screams that these men and women had stifled deep within their throats, so strong that they had seeped out through their eyes in long, salty rivulets.

It was on that day that he began to rust from the inside.

If only he had been allowed to sink. They had made so many reefs out of boats too old to be of any use anymore. Maybe under the water he could have had some chance of crushing these screams beneath the weight of heavy sleep. They settled on beaching him, like an unremarkable bit of wood, and shrill, jeering birds taunted him relentlessly, screeching and fighting to perch on his hull, covering him with their yellowish droppings before flitting off again.

He couldn't help thinking of the *Catalina* every so often, a twin-engine plane just as broken as he was. Back there, on the beach of Diego Garcia. Its nose pointed skyward, its carcass strangely slumped in the sand. At least it had served as a playground for the children.

The children. All these years later, he still retained the traces of their terrified tears. And there had been this scream, unlike any of the others. He had never heard such a sound before. He would go on hearing it until he died. This scream of a baby being brought into this world. This sound had made the ship tremble from stem to stern. He would have liked to blare his siren, to spread the joy of this moment. A baby. A baby was born within me. In my belly. I helped a baby come into this world, I sheltered a baby, I cradled a baby. But they took the baby away, the baby and all the others.

île nous reste les cartes les traces
vies voilées par l'histoire violée

île nous reste à crier à écrire
la haine imbécile
et l'histoire qui s'enchaîne

Diego ton nom sur la carte rayé
Diego amour
Diego amer
Diego à mort . . .

I'll land this, our pain: maps and traces
lives halted by a history assaulted

I'll lend this, our pen, to write, to right
their futile hatred
and the ties and tides of history

your name, scratched from the map, Diego
loving Diego
loathing Diego
nothing Diego . . .

MICHEL DUCASSE, *MÉLANGÉS*
TRANSLATED BY LISA DUCASSE

DÉSIRÉ WOKE UP WITH A START. The whole night, this boat had been talking in his head. He was obsessed. There was so much he wanted to know, to understand. But he could tell that he wouldn't be able to ask his mother all these questions overwhelming him.

He left the house quietly so as not to wake her up. Outside, the night was slowly dissipating. He walked aimlessly. A few dogs were rummaging through overturned trash cans. The streetlights were falling asleep one by one. It was only when he saw the makeshift fence of barriers around the harbor that he realized his feet had led him there, once again, irresistibly.

He made his way up the deserted promenade, which would soon welcome the horde of tourists, office employees, and other people who found themselves in Port Louis each day. Sitting on a bench, he contemplated the smooth sea stretching out beyond the wrought railing. A few greasy pieces of paper and plastic bottles had collected in an oil slick that was slowly moving across the water.

At the far end of the railing, at the corner where the wrought metal stopped and left an empty space, a woman was standing immobile. A headscarf knotted around her head. Practically a statue.

She suddenly wobbled ever so slightly. Désiré was sure of it. She had moved forward just a little, nearly imperceptibly in fact, but she was so close to the edge. He got up, slowly walked up to her.

She turned around. In her eyes was the same strange shakiness that he sometimes saw in his own mother's gaze.

CHARLESIA INVITED HIM to come see her in Pointe aux Sables. She often left the slum to go fish off the side of the jetty. In the middle of the day, the men were out at sea, and she could sit at her leisure beneath the shade of the *pongam* trees.

She spent hours talking to Désiré as she prepared the small fish she had caught through sheer patience. It was hot. She was drinking some coconut water to quench her thirst. But that wasn't easily found here. Back there, the coconut tree had been at the heart of their lifestyle. They had used every part of it, they had known how to make everything from it. Coconut-palm oil, brooms with palm-tree ribs, mattresses of coconut straw, mats woven from the leaves. Brushes with the dried husks that had a natural curve perfectly suited to the arch of their soles and which sang out on the waxed floors that the women left gleaming as they danced funny versions of the twist. In any case, they all worked for the Chagos-Agalega Company, a corporation that had leased these islands from the Mauritian government to make copra.

"Back there, we didn't need money to live," Charlesia insisted. "But the others wanted money. They sold us."

"What do you mean, sold?" Désiré replied. "You didn't belong to anyone. You weren't slaves, were you?"

The sharpness of his question took her aback.

"Huh? No, no, not at all. Not us. But apparently our ancestors were slaves. Some say that in the eighteenth century, a French colonizer in Mauritius had gotten authorization from the governor to start a coconut plantation in Diego Garcia. They say that he brought a hundred Malagasy and Mozambican slaves over, and that others had followed suit after his business started to flourish. Our history goes back a long way. They tried to claim that we were just seasonal workers brought in from Mauritius to work on the Chagos for a few months or years. Seasonal! They erased everything, denied everything, even our cemeteries, even the tombs of our forebears. As if we had somehow brought our ancestors there with us! But it all happened the other way around. It was Mauritius, the British, and the Americans who rendered us undead."

A long silence settled. Désiré toyed with a few filao seeds in the sand.

"We didn't realize what had happened to us. It was only a long time after that we understood the trade that had been made on our backs. The British and the Americans had sealed their deal. And Mauritius didn't do a thing to help us. Getting its independence was good enough."

Désiré remembered the independence celebrations at school. A happy day that as a child he had awaited excitedly.

The prospect of a free half-day, with no papers or slate, no conjugations or calculations, with sparkling limeade and French treats covered in sugar and cream, after the flag-raising ceremony and the official speech the superintendent had read aloud with a solemn accent while sweltering beneath the noon sun in his black suit.

The speech always bored them. They didn't understand much of it, but they had to stay there, in tidy rows, while sweat snaked down their backs. Snickers would always make their way through the lines as the superintendent talked about discipline and obedience and about building something which they never heard the name of because they were being shushed loudly by their teacher.

One year, his friend had pretended to faint in the middle of the speech. He had slumped all of a sudden, making sure to fall on his left side, onto the carefully tended soccer field. Two teachers had run over, one had picked him up by the shoulders, the other by the feet, and whisked him away before everyone else had been able to crowd around him and shriek in mock fear. It was a total failure, they hadn't been able to make everyone else panic enough to put a stop to the ceremony. The superintendent had kept on reading his speech with renewed fervor, and they had to wait until it was time to sing before they could let off steam: "Glo-o-ory to theeee, Motherlaaand, oh Motherland of miiiiine."

He could still hear himself bellowing the national anthem with all the school's other voices, after having dutifully practiced it in class for days on end, trying his best not to let himself be distracted by the squeaking of the flutes meant to accompany them. The superintendent directed them to sing it in French after the official version in English, "*Gloire à toi Île Mauriiiiiiiice, Île Mauriiice, ô ma mère patriiiie.*" The man had then launched into "Rule Britannia, Britannia rule the waves," in memory of the era when Great Britain reigned over the seas of colonization. We never sing about our country enough, he thought.

His country. Their independence.

Désiré recalled the photo he had glimpsed in a paper, a man with a rounded belly in his dark suit, his thick, black-rimmed glasses beneath white hair, standing in front of a far larger man with a silly triangular hat wreathed in white feathers and a red-and-white uniform. Or was it blue and white? He wasn't too sure anymore, but he retained the memory of that man dressed in gilded stripes as well as the authority he exuded. The whole scene seemed imposing, two men standing at attention in front of a pole. One flag was replacing another. 1968, the British Union Jack was being lowered, the Mauritian Quadricolor was being raised, beneath the eyes of the last British governor, Sir John Shaw Rennie, and the first Mauritian Prime Minister, Sir Seewoosagur Ramgoolam. Independent. Proud.

Back there, at the far end of the sea, a long way from the trumpets and cannon salvos, there had been his mother, his father, it had been a day like all the others of their tranquil life, a day that would be a ruinous one in their history. Their fate would be sealed, behind their backs, without a word, without even a single thought for them.

Glo-o-ory to theeee . . . Whom ought he to sing glory to today? Oh Indian Ooocean, oh mothersea of miiiiine?

"That doesn't even rhyme!" he said.

"Yes, my child, there's no rhyme to it. No reason, either. There hasn't been any ever since we were dumped on Mauritius without a thing. Without any money, without even the right to eat whatever we wanted. Here they claim that tortoise meat gives you tuberculosis! Tuberculosis! You know what that means? We should have been dead and buried eons ago! It would have done them some good just to try. We had tortoise oil and our children were hale and hearty. None of them got sick."

Désiré had never tasted tortoise meat. He couldn't say he was particularly tempted.

"But we fought to get our rights back anyway," Charlesia went on. "We had so many protests and hunger strikes. One time I got beaten up by the police and locked up. But that didn't stop us."

Yes, Désiré had heard about this battle led by women like Charlesia. He had read about it in the paper, a barefoot woman on the road, struggling against three uniformed policemen trying to pull her into their jeep.

"Oh, yes, we fought well! We laughed right in their faces!"

Charlesia had decided, along with a group of Chagossian women, to go and protest in front of the British High Commission. They knew the officials would have never let them in. They'd borrowed sophisticated clothing from their friends, and presented themselves at the door, wearing makeup, perfume, and coiffed hair as if they were requesting visas. They were let in without any trouble. Inside, they had rushed to the windows to unfurl the protest banners reading "RANN NU DIEGO!" and "ANGLAIS ASSASSINS!" that they had hidden in their purses all while they shouted "Ramgoolam sold Diego!"

Charlesia chuckled. "You should have seen their faces! And I can tell you they didn't have an easy time getting us back down! They dragged us to the elevator, and once we were inside, we just sat right down and refused to move. When the police came to try to get rid of us, we gave them a few kicks and a few umbrella jabs they wouldn't forget anytime soon!"

"But in the end did you get anything?"

"Nothing at all. Or that little. Just a small payment to Mauritius from Great Britain in the eighties. Barely enough to cover the interest on everything we'd had to borrow just to survive."

In exchange, they had been forced to sign a document that they hadn't been able to read.

"It was only much later that we found out that this paper said we were giving up our right to return. As if that could be bought or sold. As if they could just dig our umbilical cords up from where they were buried!"

"But they don't have any right . . . we need to keep fighting! Why can't we go back home?"

"Because of the war, in fact. The weapons. Diego Garcia has become one of the United States' most important military bases. Which allows them to keep the Middle East in check. They have huge planes, back there, powerful ones. They call them B-52s. Bomber planes. They killed us. They keep on killing other people elsewhere. That's what our paradise is used for."

Whistling bombs. Children crying over inert bodies. Fields of gray ruins.

"Yes, we need to keep fighting."

"I'm getting a bit old," Charlesia sighed. "Other people are starting to take up the cause now."

Désiré looked at her. At her arms and hands where a few fish scales were gleaming, a latticework of dark green veins beneath her skin, like the paths of rivers over the brown earth of a planisphere.

He paused for a moment, then said: "Meemaw, you can tell me the truth. Was life really as good back there? Really?"

She tilted her head slightly to the side, as if she were thinking over his question. Then she replied, quietly: "That's the memory we have. And memories are all we have now."

A silence. Then, in a deeper voice:

"Memory is a hook digging into your skin. The harder you pull, the more it tears your flesh, the deeper it digs. There is no way to get it out without ripping your skin apart. And the scar that grows over it will always be there to remind you of the rawness of this pain. But you will never stop coming back to that scar. Never ever. Because that's where your whole life throbs. You see, my child, it is even more alive than memory. We call it *souvenance*."

AS THEY SAT, FACING THE SEA, in the sunset's peaceful haze, Charlesia and Désiré watched the light fading away in the distance. Far beyond, they knew, lay those sprinkles of islands that a greedy hand had wrested from their memories.

Far from the din of the city bustling behind them, their gazes traced this boat that would bring them, bear them, back there, to the other side of the horizon, where the sun rose on a string of islands strewn across the sea like a prayer. Their home. Back there, in the Chagos.

AFTERWORD

Chagos: Fifty Years of Fighting
by Shenaz Patel

Isle
Exile
Copra
Trauma
Bitter limbo
Rann nu Diego
Bombard and strafe
"To keep the free world safe"
The roar of the courts erase silence
What chance do ants have against giants?
Sagren sums up the sadness of exile and loss
How was this done to the people of the Chagos?

IT SHOULD BE POSSIBLE to draw on words even when they seem insufficient for describing just how interminable, how slow, how unresolved a wound, a fight, a war has been.

For the Chagos, the year 2019 marks half a century since an entire population was uprooted and deported from an archipelago which, by dint of its position in the middle of the Indian Ocean, caught the attention of the United States. Taking advantage of the instability of the decolonizing process, the United States hardly had to convince the British to sever this archipelago from the territory of Mauritius just as its independence was being negotiated. The main island of the archipelago, Diego Garcia, was transformed into what would become one of the most important American military bases, its location allowing the Americans to maintain control over the Middle East and the global oil trade. A base that was established during the Cold War, born out of the global rivalries of the 1960s, and in the Americans' words, is still essential "to keep the free world safe."

What the "free world" fails to realize, however, is that its freedom has come at a price: that of the Chagossian population's deportation and forced exile to the Seychelles and to Mauritius between 1967 and 1973. Ever since, there has been an unending, twofold battle, which ultimately came to a head this year, 2019.

THE TWISTS AND TURNS OF DECOLONIZATION

The Chagos are a group of fifty-six islands clustered in seven atolls across the Indian Ocean, just below the Indian subcontinent. Some sources date the discovery of the archipelago back to Pedro de Mascarenhas's voyage in 1512, but the Portuguese did not establish a settlement there. In fact, it was in 1744 that France, which had occupied Mauritius from 1721, claimed ownership of these inhabited islands some 1,350 miles northeast of Mauritius.

At the start of the 1780s, Pierre-Marie Le Normand, a Mauritian plantation owner whose business included sugar and coconut production, asked Governor Souillac to give him a plot of land to produce coconut oil on Diego Garcia, one of the main islands of the Chagos. Having been granted this land, he arrived on November 17, 1783 with an estimated twenty-two to seventy-nine free men of color and slaves from Mozambique and Madagascar. He opened the way for other plantation owners and their slaves brought in to expand the island's oil production, followed by a French settler interested in fishing opportunities. In 1826, records show the population of the Chagos at three hundred and seventy-five slaves, nine whites, twenty-two free men of color, and forty-two lepers who were sent there in hopes that the meat of the turtles endemic to the archipelago might heal them.

In 1810, the British took Mauritius from France, and under the 1814 Treaty of Paris they were granted control of Mauritius' dependencies, including the Chagos. Following the abolition of slavery in 1835, the former slaves were hired to work in the coconut groves, and they were joined by a number of indentured laborers from India. By the middle of the twentieth century, the Chagos had a population of approximately two thousand.

In the 1960s, Mauritius began to negotiate with Great Britain for its independence. During the discussions that took place in 1965 at Lancaster House in London, the British were open to this proposition. However, they had one non-negotiable condition: in order for Mauritius to gain independence, Great Britain would have to retain control over the Chagos.

After some minor resistance, the Mauritian delegation resolved to accept those terms. On November 8, 1965, the Chagos Archipelago was officially separated from Mauritius and registered as a British Indian Ocean Territory (BIOT).

One may wonder why Great Britain was so determined to keep Chagos as a colonial territory even as it was in the process of decolonizing surrounding territories—the succinct answer is that this was due to the United States' interest in the archipelago. In 1962, during the Sino-Indian War, the Americans realized that they had no military bases between the Mediterranean and East Asia, which led to their interest in the Chagos.

Despite its small surface area (the three main islands barely covered twenty square miles), the archipelago offers remarkable geostrategic advantages. It is more or less equidistant from the eastern coast of Africa, the Middle East where the Arab–Israeli conflict is playing out, the portions of South Asia where India and Pakistan fought over Kashmir in the 1960s and 1990s, the far-flung Indonesian archipelagos, and the continent of Australia. Almost halfway between the Mozambique Channel off the eastern African coast and the Strait of Hormuz between the Persian Gulf and the Sea of Oman, the Chagos are ideally situated on the sea routes used for shipping oil and strategic raw materials. Moreover, the horseshoe shape of Diego Garcia, its main island, provides a deep, well-protected interior lagoon that is ideal for holding nuclear submarines.

The British weren't opposed to the idea of sharing the burden of the Western camp's defenses in this part of the world, especially since the Americans were offering them a fourteen-million-dollar discount on the Polaris missiles that they were planning to buy for their atomic submarines.

Discussions began between Great Britain and the United States, who made it clear that they wanted uninhabited islands—which Great Britain would go to great lengths to give them. With extraordinary cynicism, a British official stated in a report that on these islands there were only "some few Tarzans or Men Fridays . . . who are being hopefully wished on to Mauritius etc."; these islanders would come to be called "seasonal workers," implying that they did not constitute an actual, permanent population.

And so, in 1967, a campaign began to get rid of the Chagossian population.

The procedure was incremental. At first the inhabitants were "encouraged" to go to Mauritius to seek medical treatment or to visit friends and family. When they were ready to leave, they were told that there were no more boats returning to the islands and that they would have to stay on Mauritius.

The Americans grew impatient with this gradual relocation. In 1973, the British sent one of their supply ships, the *Nordvaer*, to carry off the last inhabitants in a single hour. Some of them were offloaded in the Seychelles, but most of them were sent to Mauritius, without any warning and without a cent to their name.

The United States then rushed to build one of their most essential military bases on Diego Garcia. It started operating on October 1, 1977, and its shores harbored the B-52 long-range bombers that were deployed against Iraq in 1991 and Afghanistan in 2001.

WHAT USE ARE INTERNATIONAL AUTHORITIES?

The Chagossians sent to Mauritius, shell-shocked by the enormity and brutality of what had been done to them, reacted by holding protests and going on hunger strikes. They received very little support at first from a Mauritius that evidently did not want to acknowledge its guilt or involvement.

But the Chagossians would not relent. In 1998, a new generation led by Olivier Bancoult—whose parents had been expelled from the Chagos when he was a child—filed a series of lawsuits against the British government that demanded official acknowledgment of the harm done to them, monetary compensation, and the right to return and to live on their archipelago.

Over the last twenty years, the eight thousand or so Chagossians have continued to pursue legal recourse in front of the English High Court and other international authorities. However, it is inevitable that there would be numerous setbacks in this battle of a small island population confronting two major world powers.

In November of 2000, the High Court in London ruled that the Chagossians' "displacement" was illegal. But after two planes hit the World Trade Center in New York on September 11, 2001, Diego Garcia became the beachhead for the United States' counterattack against Afghanistan from 2001 to 2002 and for the American military invasion of Iraq in 2003 to hunt down Saddam Hussein. In fact, the Queen of England personally issued an order that rendered the High Courts' judgment in favor of the Chagossians null and void.

In May of 2002, the Chagossians were given British passports, which was seen as a clear attempt to weaken their position. Despite their unsuccessful appeals in international courts, the Chagossians kept fighting. It was bewildering when, in 2012, the European Court of Human Rights declared that their suit against the British state was inadmissible, underscoring that, in the 1970s, the Chagossians had accepted compensation of several hundred pounds sterling from the British government.

In the interim, Great Britain undertook several other schemes. In April 2010, the Foreign Secretary, David Miliband, announced the British government's plan to create an enormous marine reserve around the Chagos. All fishing activity would be forbidden. Mauritius officially challenged this decision. In March 2015, the United Nations constituted an Arbitral Tribunal, which judged this creation of a marine park illegal. This judgment, however, did not hamper the British from moving forward with the plan.

The Chagossian suit against the marine reserve was then rejected by the British court of appeals. But, in December 2010, WikiLeaks made many diplomatic cables public, including one sent by the American ambassador in London to several departments of the American federal government in Washington, D.C., to the United States military command, and to the American ambassador in Mauritius. This diplomatic cable, dated May 15, 2009, summarized conversations between members of the British Foreign Office and American officials confirming that this project was merely a delaying tactic intended to undermine the Chagossians' claims to a right to return by framing their resettlement as a threat to the marine reserve. An irony all the greater considering that this perimeter currently contains nuclear submarines . . .

ENTER WIKILEAKS

In November, 2016, Great Britain offered forty million pounds toward social assistance programs that would help the Chagossians, insisting once more that resettlement on the archipelago was not negotiable. The British government tried another tactic on March 27, 2017: they invited Chagossians again to apply to visit their archipelago. This would be a repeat of 2006, when London had organized a one-week visit to the islands for 105 Chagossians. This time, the Chagossians refused the offer, which they viewed as a poisoned chalice and a trap. "We're inhabitants of the Chagos, not visitors," they said.

On February 8, 2018, the Chagos Refugees Group (CRG) suffered another setback, which however opened other doors. The Supreme Court of the United Kingdom rejected their challenge pertaining to the marine park, but where the appeals court had declared the inadmissibility of the diplomatic cable that Julian Assange had received from the whistle-blower Chelsea Manning and uploaded onto the WikiLeaks platform, the Supreme Court rejected that opinion and deemed the cable admissible. Even if, in its opinion, the contents of the cable didn't affect the Court's finding that the decision to create the marine park had been for illicit reasons, this decision was huge for the Chagossian case.

Julian Assange had immediately celebrated this decision on Twitter: "Big win at UK Supreme Court today in a judgment that will affect many court proceedings around the world: leaked diplomatic cables are admissible as evidence."

The Chagossians were plastered across the pages of gossip magazines when Amal Clooney was seen among the lawyers representing them in May 2018 during the London High Court's consideration of the CRG's appeal of the British government's May 2016 refusal of their right to return. In the meantime, the CRG had also benefited from the political support of Jeremy Corbyn, the Labour Party's leader.

THREATS AND REALPOLITIK

Meanwhile, another battle was being waged by Mauritius, which was arguing that its rights had been disregarded in this matter. Great Britain had flouted the Declaration on the Granting of Independence to Colonial Countries and

Peoples, which had been adopted by the General Assembly of the United Nations on December 14, 1960. Resolution 1514 prohibited any attempt to alter a country's territorial integrity at the moment of decolonization and independence. Indeed, the separation of the Chagos Islands had been censured by the United Nations, which passed General Assembly Resolution 2066, "Question of Mauritius," on December 16, 1965. It requested Great Britain to comply with Resolution 1514 as it worked with Mauritius. This request was reiterated in Resolution 2232 on December 20, 1966 and Resolution 2357 on December 19, 1967. But the United States and Great Britain paid no heed to those entreaties.

Over the last few years, Mauritius has repeatedly attempted to assert its sovereignty over the Chagos. But pragmatism and the necessities of realpolitik have consistently held sway as the two global powers have reminded the small island of Mauritius of the numerous advantageous economic and trade treaties that could very easily be annulled with a stroke of the pen. But the struggle has intensified. And, in a speech to the 70th United Nations General Assembly in October 2016, the Mauritian prime minister, Anerood Jugnauth (who had participated in the Lancaster House negotiations in 1965), caused an uproar when he called again for recognition of Mauritius's sovereignty over the archipelago and then formally requested a resolution be made on the matter.

With the United States' backing, Great Britain firmly opposed this proposition, arguing that it would create a "terrible precedent," since this concerned a bilateral dispute that ought to be negotiated between the two countries. It made no difference that a preceding opinion by the United Nations, which had given the British until June 2017 to finish talks with Mauritius, had not resulted in any concrete action. The British reaffirmed that the base at Diego Garcia contributed "in an essential manner" to regional and international stability and security, that it played a "critical" role in the fight against the most complex and urgent challenges of the twenty-first century, such as terrorism, international crime, piracy, and any other form of instability.

Those arguments were not accepted. On June 22, 2017, as a result of extensive lobbying, the General Assembly of the United Nations finally granted Mauritius's request and adopted a resolution asking the International Court of Justice (ICJ) to give an advisory opinion on the question of whether or not Great Britain had complied with international regulations on decolonization when it severed the Chagos Archipelago from the Mauritian territory. The Court was also asked to rule on the legal consequences, according to international law, of keeping the Chagos under British control—especially given Mauritius's inability to carry out a plan to resettle its citizens there—including those of Chagossian extraction. Ninety-four members voted for the resolution, sixty-five abstained, and fifteen voted against. The African Union upheld Mauritius's request, arguing the outcome of the ruling would also have significant bearing on the final processes of decolonization in Africa.

In February 2019, the ICJ adjudicated, unambiguously, that the United Kingdom's separation of the Chagos Archipelago from Mauritius was "unlawful," and that it had to end its administration of the Chagos "as rapidly as possible."

The British, however, made it clear that they had no intention of honoring this advisory opinion. The original fifty-year agreement with the United States having been renewed in December 2016; they saw no reason to alter any part of this arrangement between the two world powers. In light of this unwillingness to debate, Mauritius decided to raise the stakes by bringing the issue before the United Nations General Assembly.

THE PORTABILITY OF AN ISLAND

On May 22, 2019, the United Nations General Assembly went against intense British and American intense lobbying by voting, with an overwhelming majority of 116 countries out of 193, on a resolution recognizing Mauritius's sovereignty over the Chagos Archipelago and calling on the United Kingdom to cede the Chagos Archipelago back to Mauritius within six months. Only six countries voted against. Fifty-six abstained.

"UK suffers crushing defeat in UN vote on Chagos Islands," declared the headline of the *Guardian* that day. "The 116-6 vote left the UK diplomatically isolated and was also a measure of severely diminished US clout on the world stage . . . The scale of the defeat for the UK and US came as a surprise even to Mauritius, in view of the concerted campaign pursued by London and Washington." The paper's assessment was trenchant: "British diplomats said the non-binding resolution would have little practical impact. But it has taken a political toll, draining support for the UK in the general assembly and focusing dissatisfaction over its permanent seat on the UN security council."

The ruling is not a completely straightforward victory for the Chagossians. Even as the Mauritian side underscored the need to carry out the last step of African decolonization, Mauritius's prime minister had been clear: in regaining sovereignty over the Chagos, Mauritius would not insist that the base at Diego Garcia be dismantled. India had set this condition for supporting the Mauritian government, urging that the United States be allowed to maintain a presence on Diego Garcia in exchange for a recognition of Mauritius's sovereignty. India seemed worried that any reduction in the United States' presence in the Indian Ocean might result in a vacuum that China would quickly fill in an assertion of its increasing strength in the region. This position was a shift from India's staunch opposition to the military presence of a non-coastal power in the Indian Ocean during the Cold

War. Throughout the 1970s, the countries of the region had championed the idea of the Indian Ocean being a Zone of Peace so as to prevent any outsiders from intruding. A hope that seems to have all but vanished.

All this points to the intensification of discussions and negotiations over the "portability" of an island—relating, in economic terms, to the ability to function and to be profitable under different operating environments. And it was clear that Mauritius was willing to directly negotiate the price of leasing Diego Garcia to the United States.

Amid geostrategic stakes, political negotiations, and legal imbroglios, the Chagos Archipelago is still grappling with a past that is not yet past. A past, a history that has unthinkingly wreaked havoc on the rights of thousands of men and women. Reports indicate that Diego Garcia has recently been used as a second Guantanamo, to remove presumed terrorists from the free world and hold them in secret detention. The Chagossians, in turn, are once again caught in a bitter limbo. And, having been unwillingly deported from their homes once already, they are in fear of having their interests overlooked yet again.

No, the battle that the Chagossians have been steadfastly fighting for fifty years against this iron fist that has stripped them of their islands, of their history, has not yet been won. Nor has their freedom . . .

ACKNOWLEDGMENTS

Very special thanks to my editor, Laurence Renouf, whose clear-sightedness and friendship have been an invaluable help in writing this book, and beyond. —*SHENAZ PATEL*

Immense gratitude to many colleagues, especially Ariel Saramandi, whose shrewd answers and solutions imbued this translation with unexpected depth, and to Shenaz Patel herself, a force of nature whose voice and vision I am truly honored to help bring into English. —*JEFFREY ZUCKERMAN*

ABOUT THE AUTHOR

SHENAZ PATEL is a journalist and writer from the island of Mauritius, in the Indian Ocean. She is the author of several novels, plays, short stories, graphic novels, and children's books in French and in Creole. She was an IWP (International Writing Program) Honorary Fellow in the U.S. in 2016 and was a fellow at the W. E. B. Du Bois Research Institute at the Hutchins Center for African & African American Research at Harvard University in 2018. *Silence of the Chagos* is her first novel in English.

ABOUT THE TRANSLATOR

JEFFREY ZUCKERMAN is an award-winning translator of French books ranging from Jean Genet's *Criminal Child* to Ananda Devi's *Eve Out of Her Ruins*.

RESTLESS BOOKS is an independent, nonprofit publisher devoted to championing essential voices from around the world, whose stories speak to us across linguistic and cultural borders. We seek extraordinary international literature that feeds our restlessness: our hunger for new perspectives, passion for other cultures and languages, and eagerness to explore beyond the confines of the familiar. Our books—fiction, narrative nonfiction, journalism, memoirs, travel writing, and young people's literature—offer readers an expanded understanding of a changing world.

Visit us at restlessbooks.org